In the bitter aftermath of the Jacobite rising of 1745, a Scotsman lies imprisoned in the dreaded Bridge Hole at Inverness. His brother, Alan MacKenzie the master of Craigraven, believes there is just one last chance to obtain his release—by kidnapping the daughter of the English Governor.

Mistakenly, he seizes Caroline Candover, who is only the Governor's poor relation, worthless as a hostage. Terrified of the ruthless Highlander and with no way of escaping him, Caroline faces two alternatives. Should she risk her life by revealing her true identity or allow Craigraven to carry out his threat to force her to become his dutiful wife?

Master of Craigraven

Jan Constant

MILLS & BOON LIMITED
London · Sydney · Toronto

First published in Great Britain 1984
by Mills & Boon Limited, 15–16 Brook's Mews,
London W1A 1DR

© Jan Constant 1984
Australian copyright 1984
Philippine copyright 1984

ISBN 0 263 74591 0

Set in 12 on 13 pt Linotron Times
04/0384

Photoset by Rowland Phototypesetting Ltd
Bury St Edmunds, Suffolk
Made and printed in Great Britain by
Cox & Wyman Ltd, Reading

CHAPTER
ONE

'I'M sure there's someone watching the house.'

'Oh, Caro, what nonsense! Unless it's Jamie Preston—' Georgina sat up in bed and looked hopeful.

Caroline Candover shook her head at her cousin. 'No,' she said, 'it's not Lieutenant Preston—it looks more like a Scotsman, he seems to be wrapped in a plaid.' She stared down into the dark street below.

Georgina sank back against the pillows. 'I can't imagine Jamie in one of those blanket things,' she agreed, sounding disappointed.

Caro let fall the curtain and ran across the bare boards to climb into the high bed. 'All the same,' she said, wriggling her chilled toes, 'I'm certain there was someone there. I've had an uneasy feeling the last day or so that someone is watching us—'

'Well, if it's not my Jamie Preston, I'm not interested,' her companion murmured sleepily.

'Georgie—you shouldn't, you know. What if Uncle Candover found out that you were still seeing Lieutenant Preston after he'd warned you not to?'

The fair girl lost all appearance of sleep and sat up to stare at her older cousin, her lower lip mutinous. 'I don't care,' she cried, her voice shaking with passion. 'I l-love Jamie and I *will* see him, no matter what Papa says!'

'It could ruin the Lieutenant.'

Georgina burst into tears. 'Papa's cruel—I hate him! Just because Jamie is a younger son and poor.'

'I suppose Uncle Candover wants the best for you,' comforted Caroline, thinking privately that her uncle's ambition was more likely to influence his choice of suitor for his only daughter.

'Oh, I'll be a dutiful daughter and marry Major Pultney, his rich crony. I know I'd hate to be poor, even with Jamie, but I'll love him always.'

'Ssh-ssh. Don't cry, you'll make your eyes red and you know we're going riding in the morning.'

Mention of their usual ride had the required effect and Georgina's tears ceased flowing as she remembered an assignation made that evening.

'I'll wear my new riding habit,' she said, almost happily, 'and you, my dearest Caro, may have my old one.'

Caroline was used to being the recipient of her cousin's discarded clothes and smiled her thanks; as a poor relation she was used to being grateful and the rejected habit was not really old. Georgina had merely grown tired of her poppy-red velvet, once a length of sapphire-blue material had caught her eye. Inverness had a good trade with the Continent and even the London shops did not stock better materials than were brought into the harbour at the tiny Highland capital.

At first, when Caroline and Georgina heard that they were to join General Sir William Candover in his remote citadel where he was Governor they had been filled with dismay. The long journey had proved worse than their expectations but, at last, they had arrived in Inverness, feeling that they had travelled to a spot as far from London and as wild and uncivilised as furthest Africa. The little town, to their eyes no bigger than a large English village, had been surprisingly attractive, its tall, red stone buildings like no others they had ever seen. With the narrow streets and overhanging houses, so low that riders had to bend over their mounts' heads, the Highland town had reminded them of the most ancient parts of London.

Somewhat to their surprise they found that, only little more than a year after the battle of Culloden, the citizens of Inverness were prepared to welcome them into their society, seeming almost eager in their attempts to prove their loyalty to the Hanoverian crown. Only gradually did the girls discover that all was not as simple and easy as it first appeared; slowly they became aware that many things were hidden away from them. Half-glimpsed secrets intrigued them as they realised that many of their acquaintances lived two lives; outwardly appearing friendly to their invaders, yet beneath still holding to the old ways and fiercely loyal to their clans and chiefs.

To Caro the system seemed barbaric and yet she herself owed all she possessed to her uncle. Her mother having died giving her birth, when her father succumbed to smallpox caught while visiting his parishioners, she found herself orphaned and, but for General Candover, without relatives. Luckily she and Georgina had taken to each other and, while aware of being a poor relative, Caro had found her place in her uncle's household in the main pleasant. Sometimes she thought wistfully how nice it would be to have her own wishes considered occasionally but Georgina was a kindly, generous girl and treated Caroline like the sister she had never had.

Inverness Castle having been slighted by Prince Charles' men, the Governor had billetted himself with Lady Drummuir in Church Street, which he considered the best house in town, both the Pretender and the Duke of Cumberland having chosen to lodge there at different times. The girls could not but admire his taste. The house was close to the market place and town centre. As was usual the ground floor looking on to the street lacked windows for the safety of its inhabitants, but the rooms above were light and airy, while the outside 'turnpike' staircase led into a garden that made up for any inconvenience in living high up in the world. From their sitting-room the Candovers could look out over the green space of the garden to the wide river Ness flowing towards the sea.

The girls had quickly formed the habit of riding early in the morning, soon finding that if they allowed the weather to dictate to them, then most of their lives would be spent indoors.

Somewhat to their surprise the next day

dawned as beautiful as it only can in the Highlands, and called from their beds by the bright sun they breakfasted and dressed quickly, eager to make the most of the good weather.

'That red suits you much better than me—I can't think why I ever chose it,' Georgina commented, preening herself in front of the small mirror.

'That blue is lovely, just your colour,' Caro replied obligingly and her cousin's reflection dimpled her thanks as their eyes met in the looking-glass.

With their long curls tied back with a large, black bow and tricorn hats tilted at a becoming angle over one eye, a swirl of white ostrich feathers above and a froth of white lace below their faces, each knew that their masculine dress merely served to emphasise their femininity. Well pleased with their appearance, they exchanged glances of satisfaction and, gathering up the full skirts of their habits, clumped downstairs in their heavy riding boots.

A groom was waiting in the street with their mounts and he tossed his charges into their saddles with the ease and familiarity of a long acquaintance.

'Tomnahurich, Miss Georgina?' he asked, leading the way into Bridge Street without waiting for the answer, so sure was he of the direction they would take.

Once past the Tollbooth, where so many Jacobite prisoners had been held the previous year, and into the traffic of the main street, he fell back a little, riding slightly to the rear as they proceeded towards the river. Suddenly the now familiar feeling of being watched made Caroline's shoulder blades prickle and she glanced quickly over her shoulder to meet the gaze of a man riding a black horse close behind.

Cold grey eyes travelled over her without the least hint of friendliness, instead their depths carried a bleak antagonism that startled the English girl with the unexpectedness. For a moment their eyes held, hers wide with surprise and his narrowed to slits that appeared to glitter with menace. Abruptly he touched his heel to his mount and rode past, leaving Caro to wonder if she had imagined the strange little incident.

Watching the straight back she had to admit that at any other time she would have found the unknown rider attractive; his face had been handsome, if severe, beneath the shadow of his black tricorn, and his own unpowdered hair was that particular shade between fair and ginger that so often earned its owner the nickname of Sandy. His black horse was a fine animal and his black velvet jacket of good material and cut, making her wonder how she and her cousin had not met their owner in the small circle of Inverness society.

Concluding that he must be passing through the Highland capital on his way further north, she watched for a moment as he rode quickly over the bridge that crossed the wide river, then her attention was caught by Georgina's conversation with the elderly groom.

'Tom, is he still there,' Georgina was asking over her shoulder as they approached the long bridge, her voice a mixture of interest and apprehension.

'Yes, miss,' was the stolid reply and Caroline knew that any luckless Jacobite received scant sympathy from the English groom.

'How awful—to be confined in that dreadful place,' Georgina leaned across to whisper, her eyes wide. 'The Bridge Hole,' she declared in dramatic accents. 'I vow the very sound of it makes my blood run cold!'

'I think it's barbaric! To put a man into a hole in the structure of the bridge, where all ride or walk over him and the water only inches below.'

'It's no more than a rebel deserves, miss,'

put in Tom, with the familiarity of the trusted servant.

'I've heard tell that a woman was put there for helping a Jacobite to escape,' continued the blonde girl, guiding her mount among the busy traffic that filled the main thoroughfare of the little town.

'The Scots are less than chivalrous to their women,' remarked Caro dryly.

'Perhaps it was ordered by one of our soldiers,' suggested Georgina. 'If she was young and beautiful and he was fierce and handsome, it could be quite romantic—like a play, or a novel by Mr Samuel Richardson.'

'You'd not find it so romantic if you were the poor woman,' observed her cousin.

'Pooh! I'd open my eyes and cry and swoon a little and soon have him eating out of my hand,' laughed Georgina and clattered on to the bridge heedless of the man below.

Caroline who owned more imagination was mindful of the noise and dirt endured by the prisoner beneath the passing feet and guided her horse away from that particular area of the thick wooden boards. Soon they were across the seven arches and among the hovels and ill-kept huts of the tiny settlement clustered around the far side. Tom edged closer, his hand ostentatiously on the butt of the large horse pistol he carried in a holster by his knee, but none of the pitiful inhabitants of the squalid dwellings attempted to delay them and they were quickly through and out on the road towards Tomnahurich.

'It's a strange place,' said Georgina, gazing at the upturned boat shape of the hill that rose so abruptly ahead.

'Lady Drummuir says it means the fairy hill,' Caro told her, 'and there's a tale that two fiddlers were taken there to play for the fairy king and queen and when they came away two hundred years had passed.'

'Do you believe such things?' wondered Georgina.

Caroline looked round at the remote hills, towering blue and hazy in the distance and the sea of the Beauly Firth smooth and shining like satin to one side. Suddenly anything seemed possible. 'I—don't know,' she answered doubtfully. 'I'm sure fairies died out years ago in England, but here . . . I could almost believe in the wee folk.'

'Perhaps a fairy prince will come riding out of that oddly shaped hill and carry us off,' teased her companion and almost at once grew sober. 'Caro, my love,' she began in a wheedling tone, 'would you be so kind as to ride on with Tom a little way and meet me on the way back?'

'Georgina, what are you up to?'

The other widened her blue eyes ingenuously and clasped her hands together. 'Nothing much. I promise you . . . but Jamie is waiting by those three trees—'

The other girl turned her head and saw for the first time the horseman half-hidden in the shadows. Seeing he was noticed, he rode forward to meet them.

'Oh, Georgie, what a *wicked* girl you are!' Caroline exclaimed.

Her cousin's eyes filled with tears. 'Oh, Caro, pray be kind. You know this is the last time I can see Jamie, if I am to be married next week. *Please*, please, dearest Caro.'

While Caroline hesitated they were joined by Lieutenant Preston, who doffed his hat and bowed in the saddle.

'Ladies,' he said. 'Your servant.'

'Lieutenant Preston, I had expected better of you than this,' Caro said severely and saw a hint of colour shade his brown cheek.

'Miss Caroline, my apologies if you think I have deceived you, but I do assure you that if there was another way of speaking to Georgie I would be only too happy to take it. I would be eternally grateful if you would allow us a little time alone.'

Still the older girl hesitated, torn between the fact that Georgina was betrothed to another man and her knowledge that the proposed marriage was one of convenience only and that Georgina was young and at least fancied herself in love with the handsome Lieutenant.

'Upon my word of honour I'll take the greatest care of her,' promised the soldier, his bearing so eager and his eyes so hopeful, that Caroline found herself agreeing.

'We'll ride on a little way, Tom,' she said and set her mount into a trot, ignoring the groom's evident disapproval at her action, as he followed her.

Leading the way she skirted the strange tree-covered hill and swung her horse to the right, wondering as she rounded the far end of the mound if it was possible to circle it entirely. Coming upon the beginnings of a little pathway heading into the trees, she impulsively lifted her knee over the pommel and slipped down from the side-saddle.

'Look after my horse, Tom,' she said, handing him the reins, and, lifting the long skirts of her habit, she set off up the little track.

Knowing that Tom would only wait to tie the horses to some convenient branch before following her, she walked quickly, eager to be alone and savour this slight adventure she had found. The way was steep and the path both muddy and boulder-strewn. Soon she was out of breath and hot in her heavy clothes. Panting for breath she put one hand on a trunk of a tree and paused to look about her, only to find that the view was blocked by trees and that if she wished to see her surroundings she would have to climb higher.

Thinking she heard the groom approaching and knowing she would have to endure his scolding when he finally caught up with her, she hurried on and at last found herself on the almost bare top of Tomnahurich. No trees grew on the summit, instead the short grass was inundated by dips and hollows, so strange and mysterious that Caro could believe that each or any was the entrance to fairyland.

Climbing to the highest point, she shaded her eyes and stared down at the town of Inverness clustered below. To her right the wide sweep of Loch Ness gradually narrowed into the river that wound towards the Beauly Firth, leaving behind the tall bare mountains of the Great Glen as it sought the sea. The air was clear and she could pick out details of the town, even thinking she could identify the roof of Lady Drummuir's house by its position below the ruined castle on the prominence to the right of the stone bridge.

The breeze was fresh against her hot cheeks and pulling off her hat she tossed it on to a boulder, lifting the heavy knot of her hair to allow the wind to play on the back of her neck. Studying the panorama stretched below she gradually grew cool, while awaiting the arrival of Tom Glover. Although he was sure to be in a bad mood and bound to scold her like a child, the elderly groom had been with the family so long and loved them all so dearly that he was allowed such liberties.

The sun hid behind a cloud and Caro grew cold, suddenly realising that she had been there for some time and that Tom should have arrived long ago. All at once the fairy hill became menacing; the beauty around her was stark and frightening and a chill shiver of what could only be fear slithered down her back. Behind her a dry twig snapped and she turned quickly to face the sound.

'Tom!' she cried, relief in her voice, 'where have you been? I wondered where—' Slowly her voice faded away as her surroundings remained empty and no familiar figure emerged from the dark trees that encircled her.

The familiar prickle between her shoulder blades told her that she was being watched and she swung round quickly. 'Tom—Tom!' she called, really frightened now, and at that moment something was flung over her head and she was enveloped in thick folds of material, which stifled her screams.

Quickly her arms were pinioned to her sides and she was lifted off her feet and tossed over a shoulder. Her head thumped against someone's back as the person who carried her ran downhill. Caro could feel him dodging trees and leaping from boulder to boulder, knocking the breath from her ribcage with each step. Hot and dizzy she had to struggle for each breath and grew terrified that she would suffocate.

Suddenly the movement beneath her ceased, a few words were quietly spoken and then she was roughly thrown up to land heavily across something hard and lumpy. Almost at once a new motion began beneath her and so disorientated was she that it was some moments before she realised that she was on horseback, lying across a pair of knees.

Time lost all meaning as she fought for breath in the warm enveloping darkness, feeling as if her lungs and head were about to burst. Abruptly she was dragged upright and the material pulled away from her face. For a while she could only gasp for breath, grateful for the cold air that rushed against her hot skin. Gradually the world ceased to swim alarmingly and she recovered enough to wonder who had treated her in such an uncouth manner and why.

Afraid to look backwards at the rider, she glanced down at the arm that encircled her waist and the hand that held the reins of the galloping horse. The hands wore elegantly embroidered black gauntlets, while the arm that clamped her close to a body was clothed in black velvet that she recognised with a sense of shock. Too startled to remember caution, she turned her head and encountered a pair of cold grey eyes that were all too familiar.

Suddenly she was more afraid than she had ever been in her whole life and, without care for the consequences, she sprang into action, struggling wildly as she tried to throw herself to the ground. The arm about her tightened unbearably as the rider subdued her efforts without slowing the speed of his horse.

'Be still, Miss Candover,' he said into her ear, making no threat, but his voice so charged with menace that Caroline shivered with fear and obeyed.

When every muscle in her body ached from the uncomfortable ride, their headlong speed was slackened. For a while they had been riding over fairly open ground and now they approached a tiny cottage, scarcely more than a hovel. Stopping beside the door, her captor dropped her to the ground like a discarded bundle and jumped down himself, tossing the reins to his henchman who had just arrived.

'Soldiers!' said the new arrival succinctly, pointing into the distance, and following his finger Caro saw a line of red-coated men obviously heading for the cottage.

Without ceremony she was hauled to her feet and thrust through a low doorway into the dark, smokey interior. A few quick words were exchanged with the woman who stirred something in a pot over the central fire, and the English girl was hustled towards what appeared to be a wooden cupboard built against one wall. As her eyes grew accustomed to the darkness, she could see that the knee-high floor of the cupboard was covered in blankets and realised that the strange piece of furniture was in fact a bed.

With the realisation came a renewal of the fear she had felt earlier, turning her into a wild, struggling virago. The man in the black velvet picked her up and threw her the few remaining feet into the box-bed, forcing his handkerchief into her mouth and knotting it tightly behind her head. Dragging the stock from about her throat, he flipped her on to her back and tied her wrists together, before bundling her against the wall and heaping the bed coverings over her. Caroline heard the wooden doors close just as heavy footsteps crossed the doorstep. 'Morning, missis,' said a voice in the unmistakable accents of London town. 'I see as you have visitors. May I ask your business, sir?'

'You may indeed, Sergeant,' answered Caroline's captor in tones as English as her own. 'I have just ridden out from Inverness where I am visiting my kinsman. We hoped for refreshment, but this woman only speaks some outlandish language.'

'They mostly do,' replied the soldier and broke into halting Gaelic interspersed with English words. 'She says she only has oatcakes,' he explained to his supposed fellow countryman, 'but that you are welcome to that.'

'I am surprised that you can talk with her.'

'Oh, I generally picks up a bit of the lingo—I can parley-voo like a gentleman,' he said cheerfully. 'Well, now we've seen who you are we'll be off—I'd be back in town before dusk if I was you, sir. That's a fine piece of horseflesh you have there and the natives aren't above sticking a dirk between your ribs to steal such an animal.'

'I'll remember—and thanks for your

advice. You were very alert to notice us. Are you looking for someone?'

'Returning from patrol, sir. It's not often as we see a well-dressed gentleman in these parts and I was curious. What was it you threw to the ground so impatient like, if I may ask?'

There was a pause, then: 'Just my cloak. There it is, Sergeant, by your feet.'

There was silence while the Sergeant obviously surveyed the garment. 'I see, sir—well, as I said, we'll be on our way. What did you say your name was?'

'I didn't—but it's King, George King.'

'Very patriotic, if I may say so,' responded the soldier dryly and Caro strained her ears, hoping that his suspicions had been aroused, but after a while she heard shouted orders and then the muffled sounds of horses trotting away.

After what seemed an age, the door of her prison was opened and light spilled in as hands reached for her and dragged her to the edge of the bed. Like a doll she was roughly jerked this way and that as the gag was removed and her wrists freed.

Quite suddenly fear was brushed aside by anger, as rage at such treatment consumed Caro. A poor relation she might be, but until the last few hours no one had laid rude hands upon her. Their indifferent, ungentle touch filled her with fury and almost of their own volition her hands flew towards the grim face above her, fingers crooked into talons as she reached for the cold, grey eyes with her nails.

She saw with satisfaction two red stripes appear on either cheek before her wrists were seized and dragged down. For a moment she thought her bones would break and then she was flung aside and the man in black stood up, wiping the blood from his face. Cursing, he stared at the bright drops on his fingers, before turning his gaze to her, where she crouched like a wild animal at bay.

His look was far from kind and to hide the fear that was again gaining supremacy, Caroline deliberately fanned her anger as she lifted her chin.

'How dare you—how d-dare you treat me like this!' she raged. 'You brute, you bully . . . you odious cowardly lout to ill-treat a helpless female!'

A hint of grim amusement crept into his grey gaze. 'Hardly helpless, Miss Candover,' he said, touching his scarred face. 'I carry more wounds than you.'

Caroline grew still as her eyes widened. 'You know my name—I remember you using it before.'

'Of course. I am not given to abducting any female—I *chose* you very carefully!'

His captive shivered involuntarily. 'W-who *are* you?'

'Craigraven.'

'Then, Mr Craigraven—'

'My name is Alan MacKenzie—Craigraven is my title. Where I live,' he explained impatiently.

Caroline disdained this introduction. 'Why have you abducted me?' she demanded. 'If you hope to hold me to ransom—' She broke off as she saw by his expression that that was precisely his intention. 'Then, let me tell you Mr whoever-you-are, that you are a fool. I am not rich.'

A brown hand stretched out and it was all that she could do not to flinch away as the Scotsman ran the back of his fingers lightly down the sleeve of her riding habit, flicking the lace ruffle as he reached the deep cuff. Continuing the journey, he touched each of the tiny gold buttons that fastened the pseudo-masculine waistcoat she wore until, finally, his fingers reached the fastenings of her lawn shirt and paused beneath her chin, tilting her head backwards.

'These are not the clothes of a pauper, Miss Candover,' he pointed out quietly, 'but it's not money I want.'

Releasing her chin, he swung away to lean one arm on the doorpost and stare out blankly at the surrounding countryside. He was silent for so long that Caro began to think he had forgotten her presence, but after a while he spoke again.

'This morning, my fine Sassenach lassie, you rode over the stone bridge of Inverness with never a thought for the man imprisoned beneath the hoofs of your horse,' he said harshly.

Caroline was about to deny such insensitivity but decided that perhaps silence was more sensible and waited for Craigraven to continue.

'That man, Mistress Candover, is my brother and you are the means of his release.'

'I—*me*. But—!' Realisation dawned on her suddenly and she bit her lip on her exclamation, her mind reeling with understanding.

'Your father, the Governor, will, I'm sure do anything to secure the return of his daughter—safe and unharmed,' said the Scotsman, confirming her suspicions. 'Don't you agree?'

'Oh, yes,' she whispered, thinking that the General would hardly feel the same about an orphaned niece. She was about to enjoy the triumph of telling her captor the truth, when she realised what his probable reaction would be. Suddenly recalling all Georgina's kindnesses and remembering that her uncle had, however unwillingly, given her a home, she knew that she could not confess and let this man return to Inverness with the object of kidnapping her cousin. For a while at least, she would let Craigraven think her the Governor's daughter and then reveal her true identity when they were too far away to make his return reasonable. 'He will be very worried by now.'

'Precisely,' the tall Scot replied, 'which is why we are about to send him a little message.'

CHAPTER
TWO

'WHERE'S Tom—what happened to my groom?' Caroline asked abruptly, ashamed at having forgotten the elderly servant for so long.

'Recovering from a sore head I'd say, and no doubt trying to think of an excuse for mislaying his mistress.' Alan MacKenzie saw her evident anxiety and added, 'Rest easy, he only had a wee knock on the head.'

'He's an old man.'

'But tough. Jock here had quite a fight with him.'

The man who had ridden with them grinned and nodded at his name, but clearly had heard little of the conversation.

Craigraven studied his prisoner. 'Now, what shall we send your father as a keepsake?' he wondered as he took a lethal looking knife from his pocket.

Remembering tales she had heard of the rebels' atrocities, Caro's face blanched as she hid her hands behind her back.

Seeing her gesture the tall Scot smiled grimly. 'I was thinking more of those gold buttons on your vest than a finger or two,' he told her and catching hold of her waistcoat began to cut away the fastenings, each snick of the blade jerking her forward slightly. 'Now, Miss Candover, let's disguise you,' he said, when a tiny pile of little gold discs glistened on his palm. Looking about for something to contain them, his eyes alighted on her stock, discarded on the rumpled bedding and he knotted the buttons in it and tossed the bundle to his man.

Turning to the watching woman, Craigraven spoke quickly in Gaelic and she crossed to a dark corner of the room and produced a large bundle tied in a tartan shawl. Returning she dropped it at Caro's feet and on impulse the English girl caught the older woman's hand and appealed to her for help. The hand was withdrawn from her grasp and Caroline looked at the other for the first time, noting with surprise that the hand and face were black from the peat smoke that filled the cottage with a thick haze. Meeting the pale gaze she was startled by the enmity with which the woman stared at her, her blue eyes twin pools of hate.

'Her son was killed at Culloden,' Alan MacKenzie explained briefly, 'so look for no help from her.' His booted foot stirred the bundle at Caro's feet. 'Put these on,' he commanded. 'From now on you'll play the part of a Highland lassie.'

Caroline looked at the clothes with distaste, 'No,' she said firmly and turned away.

'You'll do as I say, whether I have to act the part of ladies' maid or no,' said a voice behind her and a little icy shiver trickled down her spine. 'Though to tell the truth,' the tone became considering, 'I dare say Jock and I would rather enjoy the exercise.'

A horrid vision of the three of them struggling and fighting around the dirt floor made Caro shudder and reach down for the bundle. 'I'll not give you the pleasure, Mr Craigraven,' she cried.

'Craigraven—just Craigraven,' she was told, and felt an inordinate sense of triumph at having found a delicate spot in her captor's armour.

Putting the knowledge away for future use, she untied the knots of the green material and inspected the contents. A full blue skirt and bodice met her eyes, with a white linen petticoat and full-sleeved shift beneath.

'Go away,' she commanded imperiously.

'For the moment,' agreed the Highlander

mockingly, 'but don't take overlong with your toilet or I'll be back to aid you!'

With the words he clapped his follower on the shoulder and they both left the little room, momentarily making the interior even darker as they blocked the doorway. With a wary glance at the silent woman, who had placed herself between the English girl and the only means of escape, Caroline turned her back and began to undress; the skirt and bodice fitted tolerably well and she was relieved to find them freshly-laundered, while the shift covered her arms in crisp snowy white which showed below the short sleeves of the blue bodice. She was at a loss to know what to do with the enormous green and blue tartan shawl, a wide leather belt with an ornate silver buckle and a length of scarlet ribbon.

With an impatient click of her tongue the dark faced woman snatched up the shawl and draped it over her head and shoulders and buckled the broad belt about her slim waist, finally pinning the shawl together on Caroline's breast with a round silver brooch with a yellow stone in the centre. Just as she finished and bent to gather up Caroline's discarded clothes, Craigraven returned and the English girl saw that he too, had changed and now wore long tight tartan trews and a short fitted jacket in the same blue material as her dress. A flat round bonnet replaced his fashionable three-cornered hat, giving him a totally different air. A length of material was wound under one arm and over the other shoulder, the thick folds held in place by a brooch much like the one at Caro's breast.

For a moment he looked her over before, picking up the red ribbon, he tied it about her forehead, pulling the black bow from her hair to allow the two strands of red to flow over her brown curls. Once more he examined her and frowned suddenly.

'Sit!' he commanded and with a hand on her shoulder pushed her back to the bed. Kneeling, he pulled off her riding boots and the white silk stockings she wore.

Astonished by his actions Caro could only stare down at his bent head, but when he took her bare foot and scooping up dust from the dirt floor began to rub it over her skin, she attempted to jerk herself free. His grip merely tightened as he continued with his task, his fingers quick and firm on her ankles and feet. Caroline had never felt a man's touch so intimately before and disturbed by the sensual feel of his hands on her, grew hot and embarrassed.

Sensing her disquiet, Alan MacKenzie

glanced up and, holding her eyes, deliberately cradled one foot in his hand, gently stroking the high instep with the ball of his thumb. Caroline's cheeks flamed as she pulled herself free and this time he let her go, showing his teeth in a wide grin as he climbed to his feet.

'Highland women prefer bare feet,' was all he said, as the English girl hurriedly pulled down her skirts, 'so you'll be sampling the delights of tramping through dust and mud and over burns and boulders.' His gaze travelled over her disparagingly. 'It's a pity you're not bigger. I might even have made you carry me on your back across water to keep my brogues dry.'

Caro stared at him in disbelief. 'I'd heard that you were savages,' she said clearly, 'but had no idea that it was the truth!'

'As it is, you'll walk while I ride,' Craigraven went on evenly.

'Without shoes! You must be mad!'

'No—just eager to keep the disguise. Highlanders ride, while their women walk beside and from now on, Miss Candover, you will play the part of my woman to perfection.'

He turned away to speak to his fellow countrywoman and Caro was silent, mulling over the ominous meaning behind his words.

She had seen a tiny black knife in its sheath on a shelf beside the bed some time ago and determined to take it if possible; now, realising the need for some means of self-defence, she reached out quickly and secreted it in the palm of her hand. It took only a second to thrust it inside the low neckline of her bodice and when she looked up the occupants of the tiny cottage were still busy about their own affairs, with no one taking the least notice of her.

Suddenly struck by the fact that the door was unguarded, Caro realised that the moment for escape might have come and without further thought seized the opportunity. The fair haired Scot was at the doorway before her, surprising her by his speed. Almost lazily he took her wrist, tossed a coin to the woman and left the cottage, dragging Caro after him.

Gone was the fine black horse that had carried them so well and in its place Alan MacKenzie's servant held the bridle of a small short-legged, shaggy animal. When Craigraven mounted the odd horse, his long legs almost touched the ground, presenting so ridiculous a picture that Caro could not suppress a snort of derision.

The Scotsman raised an eyebrow. 'You may laugh, my fine English lassie, but I'll wager this wee garron will outrun you to-day.'

Growing sober at the thought, Caro met the steely grey eyes. 'How far do you think I'll get with bare feet? Let me wear my boots.'

Craigraven shook his head. 'Your fellow countrymen will be out looking for you,' he said. 'They'll not spare a second glance at a Highlander and his family—unless the woman happened to be wearing a pair of elegant boots. No, my bold lassie, you'll go barefoot and hope the road is easy.'

With the words he bent to tuck a short length of rope under the leather belt about her waist. With the end in his hand, he nodded to her.

'Just to make sure you don't get lost,' he said pointedly, kicking his heels into the little horse's sides. 'Put your hand on my knee,' he advised.

Caroline hastily drew away from his proximity. 'I will do no such thing!' she cried, shocked at the suggestion and was jerked forward as the little procession started out.

They had not gone far when a boy stepped out of the shelter of three tall pine trees to meet them. Again quick words were exchanged in Gaelic and then Caro saw the knotted cravat that held her waistcoat buttons handed over. With a final salute the boy turned and trotted off heading back towards the low outline of Tomnahurich.

'Just to give the Governor something to think about,' observed the mounted man, following her gaze as she watched the boy out of sight.

'They'll catch him and make him tell all he knows.'

Craigraven shook his head. 'Not Lachie— he's the best pickpocket in Inverness. Your father will find the buttons in his pocket and wonder how they came there.'

'You don't really believe that this hare-brained scheme will work do you?' Caro asked, exasperated.

'You had better pray it does,' was the grim comment as they moved off again, 'for you'll not be free until my brother enjoys his liberty again.'

Caroline shivered at the finality in his voice and then her attention was concentrated on picking out the best course to follow on the rough track. At first the way was fairly easy, as it led over soft dry earth , but after a while the path became strewn with boulders and small pebbles that cut her feet and dry heather roots that scratched her bare legs. When they plunged without pausing through shallow streams it was almost a pleasure to feel the cold water splashing on her skin and the soothing mud between her toes.

To begin with the English girl rather enjoyed the unusual experience, so different from her normal existence, but as the hours passed and the distance travelled lengthened her legs grew heavy and tired. They were following the road that edged the Beauly Firth and had just come in sight of Red Castle on the further shore when the regular tap of a drum carried to their ears and a troop of Redcoats marched round a bend ahead.

Without turning her head Caro was aware that both men had tensed and felt them draw close on either side. With every appearance of ease, Craigraven rode on.

'One word, one sign from you, Miss Candover and yon brave laddie with the wee drum will meet his maker.' Moving his hand slightly, he allowed her to see the ornately decorated pistol hidden under the blanket he wore across his shoulder.

Looking at the young boy who marched ahead of his troop, resplendent in his red and white uniform, his childish face alight with pride and pleasure as he beat out a rhythm, Caro knew that she could not put him at risk and slowly let out the breath she had been unconsciously holding.

'Very good, Miss Candover. I'm glad you are sensible—I'd prefer not to kill children.'

As the groups approached each other, a heavy hand was laid on her shoulder, its weight both restraining and warning.

'Good day to you, sirs,' called Craigraven, doffing his bonnet as they drew level. 'You've fine weather for your march to Inverness.'

The Lieutenant riding at the head of the column returned his greeting, stopping beside them for a moment as his men marched past. The little drummer boy winked blatantly at Caro as he walked by and showed his prowess on the drum by adding several flourishes and tattoos without breaking rhythm. Despite her predicament, she could not restrain a smile at his masculine pride and blew him a kiss, hoping he would remember the incident later and perhaps connect it with the Governor's missing niece.

'How was the town when you left it?' enquired the English soldier, evidently keen to break the monotony of the long ride.

'Much as usual—there's a new prisoner beneath the bridge.'

Caroline held her breath at the Highlander's daring as she waited for the reply.

'Poor devil!' commented the young Lieutenant compassionately. 'I wouldn't put a dog there.'

'You're talking of a rebel against King George.'

'So I am—but he's also a Britisher, as are you and I, sir. I'll tell you plainly, sir, that I've no time for you Scots who make a pleasure out of ill-treating your own countrymen! I bid you good day, sir.'

With the words he touched his riding whip to the brim of his hat and clapping his heels into the sides of his mount he rode off to rejoin his troop.

Looking up, Caro found her captor staring after the English soldier with a somewhat nonplussed expression on his bony face. Feeling her gaze he dropped his eyes to meet hers and reading her thoughts, shrugged as his mouth relaxed into a fleeting smile.

'Obviously a man after my own heart,' he observed quietly, kicking his garron into motion.

During the short rest Caro's muscles had stiffened and as she took a step forward she realised how she ached and how cut and bruised were her feet. Looking up at the tall man comfortably seated on the little horse's broad back, she was consumed with fury at his utter indifference to her well-being and before she had thought about the consequences, she had sat down on the rough grass and folded her arms.

'I can't walk any further,' she announced, her firm tone faltering as she met the cold gaze staring down at her. 'D-drag me—beat me if you will, I can go no further,' she said, lifting her chin.

'I shan't do either,' was the unexpected reply. 'Jock here, shall carry you. Jockie, my brave laddie, take Mistress Candover up on your shoulders piggy-back style.'

The servant seemed eager to comply, but the indignity of such a position was too much for the English girl and she scrambled to her feet with a groan.

'Keep your hands to yourself, fellow,' she commanded evading his grip as he reached for her. 'No one shall treat me in such a fashion.'

'Pride goeth before a fall,' quoted Alan MacKenzie, jerking the rope at her waist so that she was brought to her knees amid the tufted grass.

Caroline was not hurt, but the slight to her pride and the obvious amusement of the two men was too much for her composure and jumping to her feet she turned towards the line of Redcoats who were almost out of view and shrieked for help at the top of her voice. As a row of distant faces turned in her direction, she was lifted off her feet, dragged across Craigraven's knees and her struggles subdued. His hand clenched in her hair and pulled her head back until she thought her neck would snap, then his mouth closed over hers, his teeth grating against hers in a rough, cruel kiss.

Faint sounds of encouraging cheers from the soldiers carried to the English girl's ears and she felt the Highlander respond by waving his bonnet above his head, but he did not lift his mouth from hers.

'They're away now, Craigraven,' came the quiet voice of Jock and at last her mouth was free, Alan MacKenzie staring down at her derisively.

Surprising him with the suddenness of her movement, she snatched her hand from his grasp and drawing back her arm to its full limit, hit the side of his face with all the strength she could muster. Fury flared in his eyes and his nostrils grew pinched with rage, as he glared down at her.

'Twice you have done what no man dares,' he snarled, his voice hoarse with anger. 'Strike me again, Sassenach, and you'll feel my belt about your shoulders.'

With the promise, he released his grip, dropping her to the ground with as little concern as if she had been a bundle of washing. Giving her into the care of his henchman, the tall Scot rode ahead, every tense muscle speaking of his outrage.

'Come along mistress,' said the soft-voiced serving man, his hand under her elbow helping her to her feet. 'It's angry you have made him. No one has struck Craigraven since he was a child.'

'He's a beast—a brutish bully!'

'He's Craigraven,' was the simple reply, as if the name set the man above all rules.

For the first time Caroline looked at Alan MacKenzie's servant and saw a man of about the same age, but small and dark, where his master was tall and fair. His face was tanned by the weather and peat smoke, but his guileless blue eyes were as bright as a Scottish Loch on a sunny day.

'You care for your master.' It was a statement rather than a question and the man nodded.

'It's die for him I would—we're foster brothers. But being English you'd not know about that. We were brought up together. He was my father's son until he was twelve and then he went to school and I was his servant.'

He spoke with a total acceptance of the order of such things, obviously feeling it as right for Craigraven to be master as it was for him to be his serving man and seeing no reason to feel any less pride in himself than did the Laird.

'What's your name? Are you a MacKenzie, too?'

'Aye, that I am and a fine name it is. Johnnie MacKenzie, that's me—only the master and my mother term me Jock.'

'I—see,' said Caro, taking the hint as she fell in beside him.

'It's what they called me as a wee laddie,' he hastened to explain, not wishing to hurt her feelings.

Caroline began to think that this courteous Highlander might be of use to her and might even help her to escape, but in the mean time he was very much more considerate of her welfare than his master had been, giving her the aid of his strong arm and helping her over rough ground and even carrying her across a stream. This last, caused an outburst from Alan MacKenzie who had allowed them to catch up with him and who had turned his head in time to see this little gallant act.

'Let her fend for herself,' he shouted, his face black with anger. 'Wasn't it her father who put my brother in the hell hole of Inverness!'

Jock set Caroline carefully on her feet before replying. 'It's a lady she is—and wouldn't I be treating your sister the same?' he answered, facing his chief, not a bit disturbed by the other's rage, while the water poured out of the open-work shoes he wore.

'Remember she's an enemy.'

'I'll not forget,' was the quiet reply and Caro knew that it was as much for her as the other man and reluctantly relinquished all thoughts of drawing the smaller Scot's allegiance away from his chief.

They walked on for what seemed like an age to the English girl until at last, apparently sensing her weariness, Jock pointed ahead and informed her that they would stay the night at Mistress Munro's inn.

'Inn,' repeated Caro incredulously, staring at the ramshackle collection of tiny heather-thatched hovels straddling the road ahead of them.

As she watched Alan MacKenzie swung himself from the back of his garron and tossed the reins to a small boy who had appeared. By the time she and Jock arrived he was seated on a stool near the fire in the centre of the living space, sipping something from a horn beaker.

Caro looked round for another seat and seeing nothing stood in front of the seated

Scotsman, her eyes stormy. 'There is only one seat,' she pointed out.

One thin eyebrow rose. 'So?' he enquired, while the pungent smell of hot whisky and honey made her wrinkle her nose in distaste. His contemptuous indolent attitude while she stood was an insult and the ready colour flew to her cheeks.

'Of course I was foolish even to imagine that you *knew* how a gentleman would behave, let alone to suppose that you would act like one!' she told him, her lip curling.

'There's a bale of straw in the corner—It would be wise to keep your mouth closed; you'll not find the English popular here.'

'It's strange how I never met a Jacobite until I left Inverness,' she remarked, with a bite in her voice as she limped away.

A large pot, with something savoury simmering in the depths, hung over the peat fire which filled the room with a thick haze of smoke. Blinking her smarting eyes Caro realised that she had not eaten since early that morning and watched with interest as a woman began ladling the contents of the cauldron into bowls. However, when she was handed one, her hunger rapidly vanished as she gazed down at a pale unappetising stew covered with a thick film of grease.

Shuddering, she put aside the bowl and horn spoon, hoping that there might be another course with which to assuage her hunger.

'It's that or nothing, Miss Candover,' came Craigraven's smooth tones. 'By the morning you'll wish you'd subdued your aristocratic tastes and eaten your fill.'

'I'd need to be a pig before I'd eat such swill,' she retorted, knocking the bowl aside so violently that it spilled its contents across the dirt floor in a sickly stream. At once ashamed of her actions, she tried to hide behind a show of indifference and turning her shoulder, ignored the other occupants of the inn.

The woman came and threw dry earth over the spilled soup, but when Caro smiled at her, her attempt at friendliness was returned by a cold, blank gaze that reminded her of the woman near Tomnahurich. Worn out by her unusual activity the English girl's head drooped forward as she fell into a doze. Waking much later, she found the interior lit only by the faint glow from the smouldering peats and raising herself warily, glanced round to find that the other occupants were all in various attitudes of sleep.

Realising that here, at last, was a chance to escape, she slowly rose to her feet and began carefully creeping towards the door. Almost as soon as she moved, fingers closed tightly about her ankle and she was held prisoner, poised between one step and the next.

'Were you away to Inverness or just to the byre?' asked a familiar voice out of the gloom.

Understanding the euphemism Caroline stood still and icily demanded to be set free. For answer her foot was tweaked out from under her and she lost her balance to sprawl full length across the man on the floor. Arms closed round her, clasping her tightly to a hard masculine chest and for a wild moment a strong heart beat out its rhythm against her ear.

'Ah, now Miss Candover, if I'd known your intentions were amorous I would have been quieter in my demands—as it is we'll have woken the others,' whispered Craigraven outrageously.

'Let me go!' With a heave and a squirm Caro fought free of the encircling arms, unhappily aware that had he really wished to detain her she would not have won her free-dom so easily, but when she would have returned to her place in the corner found that her ankle was still enclasped.

'You'll stay by me—just in case you feel

like wandering again,' her captor told her and realising the futility of struggling she was forced to accept his imprisoning fingers.

Disturbed by his nearness and uneasily aware of his grasp on her ankle, sleep was hard to find and she grew aware of every ache and bruise on her tired body, dropping at last into a fitful doze just as a grey light began to creep in at the cracks and crevices of the ramshackle building.

The next thing she knew was that the woman of the house was astir and her guests in various states of wakefulness; some rose and stumbled outside, others yawned and stretched, while a few still snored and mumbled deep in slumber.

'On your feet, miss,' came a familiar voice and turning her head Caro found Alan MacKenzie regarding her with bright alert eyes. 'We've a long way to travel today.'

'Where are we going?' she enquired, obeying his command, brushing the straw from her skirts, as she awaited his reply.

'Craigraven, where else?'

'Is it far?' she demanded, realising with dismay the tender state of her feet; swollen and sore, even to stand on them hurt her and the thought of walking to wherever her final destination might be filled her with despair.

'Far enough, lassie. Now, come outside to

make your toilet at the burn, while the mistress here sets our porridge to boil.'

Hobbling after him, Caro wondered how
she could manage the necessities of life with
circumspection, but found that the Scotsman
was surprisingly discreet, waiting at a distance while she vanished behind a group of
convenient bushes and allowing her suf-
ficient time to wash her hands and face,
before calling her to join him.

CHAPTER
THREE

THEY left the crude buildings that served for a hostelry in a light drizzle that Jock termed a Scotch mist, but which quickly soaked their clothing. The two men seemed impervious to the discomfort, but Caroline who was tired from the previous day's efforts and downcast from the circumstances in which she found herself, grew steadily more miserable with each painful, wet step.

Leaving the road, they headed away across country, towards what seemed to be a solid range of undulating mountains. As they drew nearer, Caro was surprised to see an opening among them and realised there was a narrow valley, its steep sides little more than a gorge in the bare rock. As they entered the fissure, Alan MacKenzie reined in his horse and put out his foot to her.

'Come up before me,' he commanded, reaching down his hand.

Caro toyed with the idea of refusing his offer, but weariness won over her pride and she put her hand in his as she used his foot as an aid to mounting.

'You surprise me Mr Craigraven,' she said, settling herself across his knees. 'I had not supposed you to own a kindly thought.'

'I do not,' he answered bluntly. 'With you before me we'll make better speed—and you'll arrive in better condition.'

'You make me sound like a parcel,' Caro exclaimed, incensed by his attitude. Half turning she stared angrily into his face and grew heated with rage as she read the expression with which he returned her gaze. 'That's how you think of me,' she cried suddenly understanding. 'I'm just a commodity—a means of recovering your brother!'

'What else?' Alan MacKenzie answered angrily.

'I'm surprised you bothered to take me prisoner, you could have dropped me in Loch Ness and just pretended you would hand me over in exchange. It would have been much easier.'

'Indeed it would—but then, you see, I am an honourable Highland gentleman.'

'*Honourable!* Why you are nothing more than a scoundrel. And as for being a gentleman I've met tinkers with more right to that term than you.' Beside herself with anger, she squirmed in his grasp. 'Put me down this instant. I'll not share a horse with a Scottish lout.'

Instantly his arm slackened its grip and a hand in the small of her back pushed her off his knees to land on all fours on the muddy track.

'You'll have to beg, my bold Sassenach, before I take you up again,' Craigraven warned, his face tight with anger.

'I'd rather die,' Caro told him defiantly and within a short while began to think she would.

The narrow valley widened out into a flat basin surrounded by high, bare mountains and with a wide shallow river running through it. The rough track led beside the water, following its meandering curves with scant regard for suitability of the ground it covered. Caro scrambled through high tussocks of marsh grass which cut her legs with their thin knife-like blades and over sharp pebbles and jagged boulders, until she was exhausted and only pride kept her from asking for a rest. At last, well after midday Alan MacKenzie called a halt, flinging himself from the garron to scoop up water in the palm of his hand and drink eagerly.

Panting, Caroline sank down on to the river bank, dangling her sore and aching legs

in the cold water, too tired to do more than
be grateful for the rest. Johnnie MacKenzie
came up and showed her how to mix dry
oatmeal with water, in the palm of her hand
to form an edible consistency, while his master sat aloof a few paces away. He had pulled
off his blue bonnet and the damp breeze
ruffled his curly fair hair making him seem
more human, but his expression was still
cold and stiff, and his eyes, when they happened to fall on the English girl, were bleak.

All too soon, Craigraven was on his feet
again, indifferent to Caro's reluctance to
move. She saw Jock go up to his master and
gesture towards her.

'Yon lassie's no fit—' she heard him say,
but the taller Scotsman merely looked her
over and shrugged his broad shoulders.

'Well, Miss Candover?' he said, his voice
cool, 'Will you walk—or beg?'

Caro lifted her head. 'I'll walk,' she told
him, climbing stiffly to her feet, and almost
at once the mist turned into heavy rain, that
soaked their already damp clothing.

Leaden clouds darkened the already over-
cast sky and as the day advanced, dusk
seemed to have fallen, despite the time of
year. The men quickened their pace,
obviously eager to find shelter for the night,
but Caro found the new speed beyond her

capabilities and lagged behind, until Craigraven looked over his shoulder and then
brought his mount trotting back. Pulling him
round in a wide circle, he came up behind
Caroline who was too weary to be aware of
his return. The first she knew of his presence
was when the garron butted her between the
shoulder blades with his bony nose, sending
her flying forward until she tripped and fell
headlong.

'On your feet, Miss Candover.'

Ignoring both the command and the
stamping hoofs of the pony as it danced
impatiently, Caro lay face down on the wet
ground, too tired and miserable to make any
further effort. Craigraven nudged his mount
nearer and stared down at her supine figure,
while the girl buried her face among the
sweet smelling grass, trying to smother the
sobs of sheer misery which welled up in her.

'Put her across my knees,' the tall Scot
said as his henchman joined them and Johnnie MacKenzie lifted Caro and flung her face
down over his master's lap.

Remembering the discomfort of her previous ride in that ignominious position Caroline struggled weakly, but her protests were
ignored and a hand settled heavily in the
small of her back. The peculiar jerking gait
of the little horse made her head bounce with

each step he took, while every so often Craigraven's knee came into contact with her cheekbone. Soon the odd rhythm coupled with the smell of wet horse and her captor's tartan trews combined to make her head swim unpleasantly.

'Let me up,' she cried, pulling at his ankle which was all she could reach, hanging as she was over the side of the horse, 'let me up—or I shall be extremely ill.'

For a moment she thought her pleas would be ignored, but then the grip on her back was changed and she was hauled upright. Caro hid her pounding head against Craigraven's shoulder, too ill to care that he was her hated enemy, only grateful that he was solid and firm and that she could close her eyes on the world that was gyrating furiously about her.

She must have slept for she became aware some time later, that a masculine arm was tight about her waist clamping her firmly to a hard chest and that a plaid enveloped them both in its warm folds. In her strange dreamlike world, there was something enjoyable and secure in the situation; she rather liked the arm clasping her and settled her cheek against Craigraven's jacket with a murmur like a sleepy child.

Later again, she realised that they were climbing, the garron picking his way carefully among rocks and loose boulders, as they left the floor of the valley below. The rain had stopped, but the strange luminous dusk of the Highlands was falling quickly when at last Craigraven called a halt on a small flat patch of ground that backed on to the wide mouth of a cave.

Jock accepted her from the arms of his master and as he carried her into the cave, the pony was tied to a convenient stunted tree. Obviously the cave was a well-known shelter, for dry twigs were brought out and soon a fire was burning in the entrance. Creeping nearer, Caro stretched her hands and feet to the warmth and watched as Johnnie mixed oatmeal and water into flat rounds and set them to cook on flat stones in the fire. Taking a silver flask from his pack Alan MacKenzie offered it first to his henchman and then to Caroline. Accepting it, she took a cautious sip, but even so the fiery liquid caught her throat and made her choke. However, the spirits spread a warm glow and revived her enough to make her view the prospect of supper with interest.

The hot, crisp biscuits were hard but pleasant and with the soft goat's cheese produced from somewhere made a frugal, but palatable meal. Having eaten Caro was overwhelmed by sleep, and could scarcely keep her heavy eyelids open until she had crawled into a nearby corner, wrapped her still damp shawl round herself and curled into a small ball. Some time later, she awoke and still half-asleep stared about, startled by the unfamiliar surroundings in which she found herself.

The fire had long ago burnt itself out and only the watery moon illuminated the scene; a long object lay across the entrance to the cave and only after having stared at it for several seconds did she identify it as the supine body of the faithful Johnnie MacKenzie. Recognising him, her situation and the events of the previous days returned to her with a rush of understanding and raising herself on her elbow she looked round for his master. As she stirred fingers tightened around her ankle and the shadows beside her moved.

'Cold, Miss Candover?' Craigraven enquired and she knew from his voice that he had not been asleep.

'N-no.'

'What then? Nervous?'

'A—little.'

'What of?'

'The night—you—what is going to happen,' she was surprised to hear herself say and realised that the darkness of the late hour and their peculiar situation appeared to have removed her inhibitions.

Craigraven seemed amused by her frankness. 'I'm no ogre,' he told her.

'You behave like one,' she answered and was gratified when he fell silent.

'If—you do as you are told no harm will come to you,' he said at last. 'I do not intend you any hurt—'

'Hurt!' she cried. 'You have ill-treated me, taken me from my house, forced me to walk for miles, barefoot, through boulders and mire and now you say you have not done me hurt.'

'I could have done you more,' he pointed out.

It was her turn to be silenced as a shiver shook her. 'What if your brother is not released?' she asked in a tiny voice.

'There is no possibility of the Governor refusing my request—I am quite sure he will agree to anything once he knows why you were abducted.'

Privately Caro doubted that General Candover would be so eager for the return of his niece, but naturally did not say so, and her captor went on:

'By now he will be very worried. You have vanished, no one knows where. The buttons from your waistcoat will have appeared in his pocket . . . and a letter from you, persuading him of the wisdom of complying with my demands will be the final touch.'

Deciding not to pursue the subject of whether she would write such a letter or not, Caro let the matter pass, instead asking what manner of house she could expect to find at her journey's end.

'Craigraven is a castle,' Alan MacKenzie informed her grandly.

'Oh fie! I know how you Scots exaggerate,' she told him roundly. 'Even in the short time I've been in your country, I've learnt how you call a pedlar a merchant and a school an academy. I dare say you live in a cottage, scarce better than that hovel you designated an inn!'

'Craigraven is a tower house. While, I suppose, it is not a castle in the sense Edinburgh Castle is, it is made of stone, it is a keep, and is as impregnable as we can make it.'

'Who lives there?' she asked curiously. 'And if your brother is a rebel why are you free to roam?'

'My sister and our retainers live at Craigraven. We Scots are a canny people, Miss Candover. We were careful to keep a foot in both camps, which is why I stayed at home while Rory answered the call to rise up and overthrow the Hanoverians. That way, you see, the estate was safe whichever side won.'

'Very sensible,' was Caro's dry comment. 'But somehow hardly honourable. Surely you have convictions and opinions—and what about loyalty?'

'Of course, but my first loyalty is with my people, my clan. I owe *them* my care above all other considerations.'

'If my—General Candover finds out that you have abducted me, all your machinations and careful staying at home will have done you no good at all.'

She spoke quickly the thought having just occurred to her, but following the matter to its logical conclusion she suddenly sat upright and stared down at the man beside her, rigid with shock.

'You—d-don't intend to return me do you?' she said, her voice scarce above a whisper.

Craigraven moved and she saw his face a white blur as he turned to study her.

'What, then—will you murder me and leave my body on some desolate spot?'

His teeth gleamed as he smiled. 'I'm not a savage, miss,' he said softly. 'There is always a ship to the Indies—and slaves, so I've heard, very rarely find their way home.'

For a moment she was still, every muscle

tense as his words sank in, then he moved and she saw his eyes glisten in the darkness, and realised that he was watching her. With a half-smothered cry of fright, she jumped to her feet before he could stop her and taking a flying leap across the sleeping figure of Johnnie MacKenzie, was out of the cave and running for her life.

Although she put every scrap of energy into her effort to escape, before she had gone more than a few yards and before she had even left the flat land that marked the entrance to the cave, hands snatched at her and she was borne to the ground by the weight of a body. Rolling and squirming, she bit and kicked like an alleycat, fighting instinctively. Her hooked fingers clawed for Craigraven's eyes, but before they reached their target her hands were imprisoned and forced down on either side of her head.

'Bonnie lass,' whispered the man kneeling over her, panting and yet with something in his voice that made her shiver, 'did no one warn you of the dangers of fighting with a man?'

With the words he bent his head, his mouth seeming to swoop on hers. His lips were hard and demanding, with no thought other than his own pleasure, and with a pang of very real fear, Caro recognised the mounting passion. Realising the folly of continuing to fight him, she forced herself to relax, even attempting to return his kiss. With an indistinct murmur, he released her wrists to run his hands over her trembling body and the moment she hoped for was hers; cautiously, so as not to attract his attention she slipped her hand into the neck of her bodice and closed her fingers over the little black knife that nestled between her breasts.

In one single movement she had freed it from the sheath, drawn it out and plunged it into her attacker. He stiffened with a gasp of pain, but instead of freeing her, as she hoped, he sat back on his heels still across her body and seized her hand as she raised it to strike him again. Using his strength he broke her grip on the bone handle and tossed the knife aside, before dragging the cravat from his neck to staunch the blood already seeping through his sleeve.

'Jock—Jock,' he called, rising unsteadily to his feet. 'Come here—the vixen's stuck a *sgean dhu* into me.'

Before she could scramble to her feet, his henchman, who had been awoken by the noise, arrived and running her across the grass roughly thrust her back into the depths of the cave, sending her tumbling back against the far end with a force that jarred her teeth.

'Come out and it's dead you'll be,' he snarled at her, his accent so ferocious that she subsided, believing his threat.

Watching from the shadows, Caro saw him tending his master's wound and shuddered at her own action, wondering at the way civilised behaviour vanished under personal attack. Hugging her shins, she rested her head on her knees and fell into a fitful doze, waking to the early grey light of dawn to find that the men were already astir. Alan MacKenzie was below the cave, stripped to the waist as he washed in the river, while Johnnie was busy about the camp site, packing away their belongings and removing all signs of their presence.

'Away to the burn,' he said seeing she was awake. 'Himself's down there to keep an eye on you.'

There was no friendliness in his tone and he scarcely looked at her as he spoke. Caro realised that by her action of the night before she had forfeited any kindness he had had for her and suddenly felt very lonely. Silently she rose to her feet and made her way slowly down to the shallow river. Craigraven looked up when he heard her approach, and stood watching her until she drew level. For a few seconds they exchanged glances, searching each other's face as if meeting for the first time.

Then, still without a word, he gestured her to the water and with a curious half-bow, gathered up his clothes and left her. Turning her head, Caro watched as he walked away, noting, with an unexpected interest, that his back was both broad and brown, speaking of hours spent shirtless and that his waist and hips were narrow under the tight tartan trews. Ashamed of her unfamiliar interest in a man's body, the English girl hurriedly turned away and began her own toilet.

Washing her feet in the cold water, she was both surprised and somehow gratified to find how much damage they had sustained during her long trek. Swollen and bruised they were covered in cuts and scratches, her attention seeming to make them more painful and as she returned to the waiting men, she could hardly hobble for a sharp stabbing in the ball of her foot.

'I think I have a thorn in my foot,' she said, flatly.

Craigraven looked at her, then pulled his shirt over his head, hiding the rough bandage around his left arm. 'Sit,' he said, tucking the folds into the waist of his trews and as she did so, crouched down in front of her, taking her foot in his hands.

An unfamiliar, unidentifiable feeling shivered its way through Caroline at his touch and involuntarily she jerked her foot away.

'I won't hurt you,' he said, mistaking the reason, and indeed his hands were surprisingly gentle as he examined the sole of her foot.

Suddenly he bent his head and put his mouth to her skin. The unexpected action made Caro catch her breath, thinking he was kissing her, and even when she realised that he was sucking out the thorn, she found to her astonishment that the feel of his lips filled her with an unfamiliar excitement.

Her lips parted as her breath caught in her throat. Aware that the colour was burning in her cheeks and afraid that he would read her response in her face, she lowered her head and studied her hands tightly clasped in her lap. After a while that could have been an age or only a few seconds, the bitter-sweet contact was removed and fingers plucked out the thorn.

'You can look now, Miss Candover,' Craigraven said dryly, 'the operation is over.'

Caro opened her eyes and immediately wished she had not, the Scotsman was kneel-

ing on one knee in front of her, his eyes on
her face, his hold on her foot almost, but not
quite a caress. Hastily, she snatched her foot
from his grasp, and smoothed down her blue
skirt, unhappily aware of the brilliant pink
that washed over her in waves of heat.

'My dear lass, this is not the first time I've
performed such an action,' he told her,
amused.

'Maybe not—but it's the first time anyone
has rendered *me* such a service,' she
answered with asperity, hiding her ill ease
behind a show of temper.

'Away with you—you liked it.'

Caro quivered with outrage, furious at the
truth of his statement. 'You, sir, are no
gentleman!' she declared.

'And you, miss, are a silly wench. Would
you rather I'd left it there?'

'You could have been more—respectful.'

Alan MacKenzie made a scornful noise
deep in his throat and climbed to his feet;
their moment of amity was over and his eyes
as he looked down at her held their former
coldness. 'When I feel you are worthy of
respect, then I'll give it you,' he said curtly.

Without another word, he jerked her to
her feet and as she came upright tossed her
over his shoulder. Caro had time to notice
that the wound she had inflicted the night

before seemed to incommode him not at all and then she was being thrust up on to the back of the garron.

'Put your leg over,' Craigraven commanded impatiently.

'Ride astride!' she exclaimed, shocked at the thought. 'I will do no such thing.'

Her foot was seized and flung over the pony's head, heedless of the disarray to her garments or to the fact that she nearly fell over backwards. Aware that her legs were bare to above the knee, Caro thrust at her skirts and glared at the man below. Quirking one eyebrow he met her furious gaze and realising the futility of giving vent to her anger, the English girl lifted her chin and stared ahead, fuming with suppressed rage.

'You're learning—you're learning. We'll soon have you a dutiful Highland chattel.'

'*Chattel!*' Stung, she turned to stare at him. 'If I had the little black knife again, I'd show you how much of a chattel I am. Your women may be meek and—and chattelish, but I am a freeborn English woman—and quite different.'

'We'll see,' was all he said, but the curt reply made Caro shiver with its menacing brevity.

Craigraven swung up behind her, his

proximity making her tense and stiffen each muscle as she felt the long length of him against her body. His arms came round her waist to hold the reins, making her feel like a prisoner in his embrace. Try how she would to keep a reasonable distance between them, the uneven gait of the tiny horse threw them together until she could bear the contact no longer and demanded to be set down.

'On those feet? Losh, woman where's your sense? We're doing well enough—if only you didn't remind me of my sister Christian's wooden dolly, I'd like it fine.'

Ignoring his deliberately broadened accent, Caroline picked out the matter that interested her. 'Christian?' she repeated, questioningly.

'Aye—here we use it as a female name and isn't my Christian the fine, bonnie lassie!'

For the first time since she had met him, Caro heard affection in his softened tones and put away for future use the knowledge that he was fond of his sister.

'Did you think it was to a house of men you were going?' Craigraven went on. 'No wonder you weren't over-keen. I dare say you thought we'd set you to the washing and cooking—before we sold you off to a sugar planter!'

'I think I'd prefer to be knocked on the

head and dropped in a bog,' she told him soberly.

'Well, it's not come to a choice yet, but I'll remember your preference if the necessity arises.'

Caro thought his voice held a hint of a teasing note, but realising she must be mistaken the now familiar shiver of dread slid icily down her spine.

'Don't worry—your father will be only too eager to exchange my brother for you,' reassured the Scot, feeling her shiver. 'You only have to be patient—and do as you are bid.'

'When will you hear from my—from General Candover?' she asked, wondering how much longer she could play out her masquerade.

'Not for some while. You have to write him a suitably fearful letter yet—but we'll let him worry for a while longer. Rory's not due to appear before him until the end of the month so we have plenty of time.'

There was a pause that could only be described as expectant and Caroline found herself waiting anxiously for him to speak.

'For a young lady due to be married next week you seem extremely uninterested in the postponement of your wedding,' Craigraven remarked thoughtfully.

'I could see no use in mentioning it,' she

said hastily, eager to cover her forgetful mistake. 'After all, I am quite sure my pleas would make no difference to your plans.'

'You begin to understand me—but all the same I should have thought that an eager bride would have spoken of the happy event.'

'I have no wish to wed Major Pultney,' she said shortly, 'so if you think to use that as a lever to ensure my compliance, you are sadly mistaken.'

'An arranged match, was it?'

She half-turned to glance over her shoulder. 'Don't tell me you Highlanders don't have such things, for I've lived long enough in Inverness to know perfectly well that you all marry for gain—wealth, land and position mean as much to you as they do to us.'

She spoke with unconscious cynicism, all the disillusionment of her years as a poor relation coming to the fore. Craigraven's eyes narrowed as he looked thoughtfully at the proud set to his passenger's head. His grey eyes were puzzled as if he was surprised by her attitude. He would have spoken, but at that moment Jock, the servant, gave a whoop of joy behind them.

'Craigraven!' he called. 'It's home we are and isn't it beautiful, just.'

Following his pointing finger Caro gasped in astonishment and had to agree with him; perched high on an outcrop of bare rock, caught in a shaft of sunlight that struck from between the grey clouds, was a stone tower, burnished to brilliant white by the ray of sunshine. Around it the countryside sprang into colour, the sparse trees and grass more green than the English girl had ever seen, the rocky mountains and far hills as bright and delicate as if they had just been painted.

As they watched something white fluttered from a window high above the entrance and Craigraven raised his arm in return, before kicking the garron into a quicker pace. His wild Highland whoop echoed across the surrounding hills and suddenly the sun vanished draining the colours from the scene, until its beauty became harsh and cruel. Cold fingers of apprehension clutched at the English girl's heart as they rode up to the tall tower which now appeared grim and fortress-like.

For the first time her true position was brought home to her and her fears, which she had been able to put aside on the journey, grew overwhelming. More fearful of the future than she cared to admit, she approached Craigraven Keep and wondered what the days ahead would hold for her.

CHAPTER
FOUR

A HIGH stone wall surrounded the keep and at one time must have served as a means of defence, but as they rode under the arched gateway, Caro saw that now it formed a courtyard with stables and outbuildings built against two sides. Beyond the keep itself she caught a glimpse of an enclosed garden, with a surprising amount of colour for so bleak and exposed an area.

Craigraven dropped her into Jock's arms and swung to the ground, tossing the reins of the garron to a waiting, barefoot boy and made his way to the woman waiting in the doorway of the keep.

'Well, Morag,' he said, grinning broadly, 'here we are and with the merchandise we were after.'

The woman shot Caroline a quick look. 'So I see,' she said disapprovingly in a broad accent, 'and it's hoping I am that it works out the way you want.'

Alan MacKenzie ignored her disparaging

remark and asked after his sister. 'How has
Christian been while I was away?'

Morag shrugged, her expression clouding.
'Not so well,' she admitted. 'The lassie
misses you.'

'Has she left her room at all?'

'No—what she needs is a friend of her own
age. Someone to give her confidence.'

'Campbell Frazer is willing.'

'She's no over fond of the man, as you well
know.' The tone implied that its owner
agreed with Christian's sentiments.

'She used to be fond enough and I've no
quarrel with my factor, so we'll have no
women's fancies held against him,' Alan
MacKenzie replied sharply, turning back to
where Caro stood behind him, listening to
this exchange. Reaching back he took her
elbow to draw her forward. 'This is Mistress
Morag, who sees that my house runs
smoothly. You will do as she says.'

As if there was no more to be said upon
the matter he turned away, but the housekeeper's voice stopped him in the doorway.

'Is she to be kept close?' she asked dourly.

Craigraven ran his eyes over his prisoner's
wilting figure. 'Close enough,' he said,
'though I've a feeling you'll be having no
trouble with her for a while.'

Mistress Morag followed his gaze and made a tsk-tsk of disapproval when she saw the state of Caroline's feet. 'Poor wee lassie,' she exclaimed, 'it's savages she'll be thinking we are. Could you no treat her better than that, Master Alan?'

'Och, take her away woman. It's necessary to be hard at times, besides she's well able to take care of herself. Ask her how I come to have a hole in my arm!'

As he left them, the Scots woman turned enquiring eyes upon the girl. 'Well, miss?' she demanded.

'I—had to defend myself with one of those little black knives,' Caro told her, thinking it better not to prevaricate.

A gleam of amusement showed in the large-featured face. 'It'll be the first time Master Alan's had his advances refused,' the other commented dryly. 'Ah, well, it'll no do him any harm to learn that his charms are no always welcome. Come with me and we'll see about those poor feeties of yours.'

The main part of the ground floor seemed to be taken up by store-rooms while the guard-room was beside the stairs in the round corner tower. Above were low ceilinged rooms, used as the housekeeper's room and the maidservants' bed chamber. The narrow, twisting staircase carried on to the floor above, but there it was stopped by a strong, heavily barred door.

'That's the family's quarters,' said Morag indicating upwards with her head. 'Here's my room and beyond is where the house-lassies bide.'

The low, vaulted room was surprisingly comfortable, with wooden shutters at the tiny windows and an arched fireplace in one wall. A bed was piled high with blankets and pillows to serve as a seat and the house-keeper gestured to Caro to sit there while she busied herself, pouring water into a shallow bowl from a kettle which had been steaming over the glowing peats.

Bending her rheumatic knees she knelt to bathe Caro's cut and bleeding feet, her touch surprisingly sure and gentle as she patted and dried.

'There now,' she said, applying salve. 'I'll just away and see if Miss Christian has a pair of stockings and some shoes to fit you.'

'Why does she stay in her room?' Caro asked when the older woman returned bearing white cotton stockings and a pair of black buckled shoes.

Morag glanced at her under her eyebrows. 'Didn't she have a fall from a horse? And didn't she break her leg and it not setting straight?'

'Oh—I see,' said Caro thoughtfully. 'I'm sorry. Will I meet her?'

'I'd say it depends on many things, miss. How you behave, what the master decides and how Miss Christian feels. As it is, you're to have a chamber on the top storey.'

Caro contemplated her hands, twisting in her lap. 'Am I to be a prisoner?' she asked, in a little voice.

'The key's to be turned, if that's what you mean,' the woman told her, 'but Craigraven's no a bad man. A wee bittie quick-tempered and used to being master. Mind his words and do as you're told and you'll no come to any harm.'

She led the way upstairs again and Caro found the family's floor surprisingly elegant. As the building rose higher, so the windows appeared to become progressively larger and here they were of a good size, giving wide views of the surrounding hills. Mistress Morag did not pause, but crossed the big room quickly, barely giving Caro time to realise that the furniture was as elegant as its surroundings.

In the far corner was another door, which opened to a new stairway, again in a turret of its own. Two quick twists and an arch gave on to a little lobby with several doors in it, but putting a key into the lock of the door which closed off the rest of the stair tower, the housekeeper flung it open and gestured to the English girl to enter.

Caro did so reluctantly and found herself in a curious round room. A little bed stood in the centre of the stone floor, while a wooden chest with a china bowl and jug on it were the only other furnishings. Entirely made of stone, the room struck chill to Caro and she saw that the narrow windows were uncurtained, not even owning shutters to close out the cold air.

Mistaking her shiver for apprehension Mistress Morag tried to comfort her. 'You'll no be alone up here,' she said. 'Miss Christian's room and the family sleeping quarters are just across the landing.'

Recognising the kindly tone, Caro seized on the Scotswoman's good nature and caught her arm impulsively.

'Mistress Morag,' she cried, looking pleadingly into her face, 'you must help me. Mr MacKenzie was wrong to abduct me—believe me it will do his cause no good. If you help me to escape I promise to make no trouble for him—'

'Now, now lassie, dinna fret yourself,' the older woman said, patting Caro's hand. 'How could I help you—even if I wanted? If I let you out of the castle you'd never find your way out of the glen without someone to guide you and you can be sure that all the men here are loyal to Craigraven.'

'I'd go alone.'

'You wouldn't be the first to die in the hills.'

Caro shivered at the finality in the woman's voice and involuntarily imagined a pitiful heap of whitening bones scattered on the sparse grass.

'Someone surely—' she began desperately but Mistress Morag cut her short.

'No one will go against Craigraven. Apart from the loyalty they owe him, they all know better than to cross him. He isna the man to anger lightly, and that you'd best remember my fine lassie.'

With a nod to emphasise her words, she pulled the door to behind her and Caro heard the heavy key turn in the lock.

Feeling more alone than she had ever felt before, she wandered to peer out of one of the three windows that were spaced around the encircling wall. Below was the walled garden she had glimpsed before and again she was surprised by its fertility; low, neatly-trimmed box hedges protected the flowerbeds, kale grew in neat rows and fruit trees were trained against the tall stone walls. Stone seats and a statue completed what could easily have been a garden belonging to an English manor house.

Voices attracted her attention and Caro hastened across to the opposite window and found herself looking down into the courtyard. As she watched Alan MacKenzie's easily recognisable figure appeared from the far corner of the building and by craning her neck she could just see the main doorway. He was speaking to a man behind him and the English girl waited with interest to see who would step out after Craigraven.

A head of bright ginger hair was the most noticeable feature of the other man; beside the Laird he appeared short and slight and the kilt he wore was a different colour from MacKenzie's tight-fitting trews. They seemed pleased to see each other and discussed something animatedly for a few moments, turning to look up at her tower before, laughing, they walked off together.

She found out who he was later that day; she had fallen asleep and been woken by the door opening and Morag standing in the entrance gesturing to her to follow. Smoothing her hair and skirts Caro did so and was led down the winding stairs into the big room. To her surprise the long table was laid and three people were already seated.

'Did you expect to starve?' asked Craigraven with grim amusement as her startled gaze travelled over the scene.

'I had not expected such—splendour,' she retorted, not hiding her surprise at the lavishly spread table and the fashionable rich clothes worn by Craigraven and his companions.

She was gratified to see that her shaft had struck home as two spots of colour appeared on his high cheek-bones.

'We are Scotsmen—not savages, Miss Candover,' he told her cuttingly.

She smiled brightly. 'Really? I had not known. From the treatment I have received, savages would seem quite apt!'

'You may believe your nationality owns the prerogative on good manners, but you are sadly lacking in common sense, Miss Candover. Only a hare-brain would seek to quarrel in a position such as yours.'

Recognising the truth of his words, Caro glowered silently and into the silence a new voice spoke.

'If you and the lady have finished Alan—' put in Christian MacKenzie quietly and Craigraven turned to her at once, his gaze gentle.

'This is General Candover's daughter,' he told her. 'My sister, Christian, Miss Candover.'

Caroline curtsied, but the other girl did not rise from her chair, instead nodding acknowledgement while they exchanged examining glances. The English girl saw that Craigraven's sister was about her own age and resembled him, but where his fair hair was tightly curled, hers was blonde and lustrous. Her face was pale and her expression sad, while her grey eyes so much like her brother's were shadowed. Caro remembered Morag's tale of a riding accident and her eyes slid to the other's voluminous skirts.

Following her gaze Christian flushed and her hand fluttered over the pink satin folds. At once Caro was contrite and rushed to make amends.

'I am sadly out of style,' she told her, trying to laugh as she indicated the plain woollen dress she wore. 'If I'd known I was to go a-visiting I would have brought a suitable wardrobe, but your brother gave me no time to pack and paid little heed to my protests.'

She was rewarded by a flickering smile on the other's sober face and felt her own heart lift; if only she could find a friend in the keep, her enforced stay would be more endurable.

'You have forgotten me Craigraven,' said the man on the far side of the table.

He had risen to his feet at Caro's entrance,

but she had scarcely spared him a glance, all her attention had been focused on Craig-raven and his sister. Now she looked at him fully and saw that it was the person she had seen from the turret window.

'Campbell Frazer,' said Alan MacKenzie. 'My friend and factor.'

'Factor?' the English girl repeated the unfamiliar word.

'Steward, you would say, Campbell cares for my possessions as if they were his own.'

Caro sensed rather than saw the Scots girl make a quickly controlled movement and wondered a little at her reaction to her brother's words. Following her eyes she saw that the gaze the other had turned on the red-haired factor was no kindly one and put the matter away for future use as he made a gallant bow to her.

'May your stay with us be as happy as possible,' he said, holding the chair for her as she seated herself at the table.

The meal consisted of the usual boiled mutton and kale, which Caro was fast learn-ing to be the Scots' staple diet, but followed by an elaborate course of desserts; jellies and tarts which surprised her by their pro-fusion. She noticed with interest that, while Campbell Frazer tried to engage Christian in conversation, addressing several remarks to her, she answered him in monosyllables, refusing to be drawn, but replied happily enough to her brother. Caro, herself, found the factor to be surprisingly attentive to herself, his light brown eyes holding a degree of unspoken sympathy and understanding. Marking him down as a possible ally, she set out to charm him, ignoring Craigraven until an amused drawl was addressed to her.

'Campbell was ever one for the ladies, Miss Candover,' smiled Alan MacKenzie, watching the candlelight strike red sparks from the liquid in his glass. 'Don't trust him—I am assured that only heartbreak lies that way.'

'I am sure that a little civilised conversation will not break my heart, Mr Craigraven.'

He bared his teeth. 'Just Craigraven, if you please,' he snarled to Caro's delight.

'I *must* try to remember your little foible,' she told him sweetly. 'I see how it irritates you, MacKenzie.'

Grey eyes shot furious icicles across the table at her, but the factor spoke quickly into the explosive situation, suggesting that Christian might play for them, and after a smouldering glance at Caro, Craigraven offered his sister his arm and led her across to a pretty little harpsichord. Noticing that she walked with difficulty, dragging one leg, the English girl felt her ready sympathy rise and wondered anew at the accident which had caused her disability.

'Sing for us, Christian,' begged Campbell Frazer, but the Scots girl shook her head and broke into a lively jig.

The factor was not abashed. 'Next to a song I love a dance,' he told Caro and proffered his arm.

About to refuse, she saw that Craigraven was glowering his disapproval and immediately accepted the other man's offer.

'You will have to teach me the steps,' she laughed.

'My pleasure,' he told her, squeezing her fingers, as he looked down at her.

Used to English country dances Caro did not find the steps too difficult and soon was treading the intricate measure with confidence. Christian concentrated on her music with bent head, carefully avoiding the factor's eyes, though he obviously sought her approval. Soon the English girl's feet began to protest at such usage so soon after her long walk and she made her excuses to return to her seat.

By mutual consent and with so few words that it was clear to Caro that such a happening was by no means unusual, the two men took down two long swords from the wall above the enormous fireplace, and, first saluting each other with great ceremony, placed them across each other on the floor. Christian began to play a wild measure with flying fingers and the men began a strange dance, their bodies still and upright, but their feet flying, heel and toe at great speed. For all the quickness of their movements they were both so nimble and light, that Caro watched in astonishment and when the music stopped and they gravely bowed to each other, she could not resist breaking into involuntary applause.

'Oh, bravo—bravo!' she cried.

'Have you not seen a sword dance before Miss Candover?' asked Campbell Frazer, panting slightly.

She smiled at him. 'My education is obviously sadly lacking.'

'I have no doubt that you are well able to dance a minuet,' observed Craigraven, making her turn to him in surprise, her eyes widening as she saw that he was holding out his hand.

As if at an unspoken command his sister played the opening bars of a well-known tune and to her amazement Caro found herself putting her fingers on his as she rose. The music was slow and stately, giving her plenty of time to observe her partner as they parted and paused, turned and came together again in time to the rhythm. She was disconcerted to find that he seemed determined to hold her eyes, his own grey gaze seeming to seek her face at every opportunity.

Her fingers trembled in his light grip as she realised how attractive this enemy could be when he set himself out to charm. Now she was the one carefully to avoid a gaze, while her head was deliberately high and an artificial smile played brightly about her lips.

'Shy, Miss Candover?' whispered a voice in her ear when the intricacies of the dance had brought them close together. 'I would not have expected it of you—after all our time together.'

Caro missed a step and his fingers tightened and one arm encircled her waist as she came to a standstill.

'I—am tired,' she said, half turning towards the chair she had vacated, but he made no movement to release her.

'Afraid, Miss Candover?' Craigraven suggested in her ear.

'Indeed not!' she said indignantly, looking fully at him for the first time since they began to dance. 'You should know better than that.'

Their eyes held and seconds seemed like

hours while the others in the room faded into insignificance. For a few moments they could have been totally alone and then Caro broke away, walking quickly across to one of the long windows. Standing in the deep embrasure, she leaned her head against the folded shutter and gazed out at the dusk-filled night.

'I intend you no harm,' Craigraven said behind her and she realised that he had followed her. 'I—would not have you afraid of me.'

His voice was sincere and Caro found his changed treatment and nearness strangely disquieting. Unable to move away in the enclosed space she stared at the window, seeing the room and its occupants behind reflected against the black panes of glass, almost like a stage play. Dispassionately she watched the red-haired man bend over Christian MacKenzie to whisper something in her ear as she sat at the keyboard and saw Craigraven's sister stiffen and move away from his proximity as, ignoring him, she began to play a sombre melody.

Hands rested on her shoulder, warm through the cloth of her bodice and she shivered a little at the Laird's touch. Lifting her eyes, she studied his reflection in the dark glass only to find that he was returning the action. Somehow the fact that their gazes were once removed made the act impersonal and she was in no way discomposed to meet his querying grey eyes.

'Cannot we be friends?' he asked above her head, his breath stirring her hair.

'Friends!' she could not hide her astonishment; having imagined herself and the Scotsman many things to each other during the last few days, she was surprised to find an aspect she had not even considered.

Her reaction amused him and a smile flickered across the reflected face as his grip on her shoulders became almost caressing. 'Why not?' he asked, watching her. 'You will be with us for some time yet. Why not make your stay as pleasant as may be? Give me your word not to attempt to escape and you will be treated as an honoured guest.'

Lowering her chin to avoid the searching eyes, Caro considered the proposition. While having no real intentions of keeping a promise given under duress, she viewed the situation from all aspects before, deciding that it could only do her good, she gave her word without compunction.

'Good—now I shall not have the odious necessity of locking your door at night.'

Wondering if he was teasing her, she lifted her head to meet an expression she could not read and, disconcerted, rushed into speech.

'I would be friends with your sister,' she said and with the words realised she was admitting the truth; there was something interesting about the quiet Scots girl. Caro felt that her remote manner would be worth breaching and that once won her friendship would be worth owning.

'Christian chooses her own friends,' Craigraven told her. 'I will not—cannot—influence her in such matters.'

His eyes were on Campbell Frazer as he spoke and again the English girl was aware of undercurrents in the atmosphere that interested her.

'Mr Frazer would appear to wish to number himself among them,' she commented quietly.

'He is one of my oldest and most trusted friends—when I am away he has charge over my possessions and I have every confidence in his management. Marriage to him would be very suitable and now that she is—'

Craigraven broke off, realising that his chagrin with his sister had led him into saying more than was wise to someone who clearly would not have his interests at heart.

Caroline was surprised to feel a flash of anger on the part of the other girl. 'Miss Christian is obviously an accomplished and attractive young lady,' she found herself saying heatedly. 'Any man would be lucky to have her for a wife.'

Craigraven's smile was genuine and his expression kind as he took Caro's hand and carried it to his lips. 'I agree,' he said. 'Only not all see beyond the disability which she hides behind.'

'How long has she—I mean, can nothing be done? It does not appear *too* bad to me, more a limp than anything worse.'

'It happened about a year ago. We were going riding and she flouted my rule and mounted my horse, who took off. A girth broke and she took a fall, breaking a leg. I believe that with exercise it would improve, but since then she has shunned company, shutting herself in her room.' His eyes ranged speculatively over Caro. 'She needs a friend, Miss Candover—someone who could persuade her to take up life again . . .'

'Have you no suitable relative?'

He shook his head. 'We have a dearth of kinswomen at the moment—marriage to Campbell would be the answer.' He eyed his sister sombrely. 'I'll bring her round to seeing sense in time.'

Caro spared a moment's sympathy for the other girl before her thoughts were returned to herself by Craigraven's next words.

'Which reminds me—it's time you were after writing a note to your father. The poor man will be growing anxious—'

'I'm away to my bed, Alan,' came his sister's voice. 'It's late and doubtless your guest is needing her rest, too.'

Thankful for the interruption, Caro sent a smiling glance across the room, wondering if the announcement had been deliberately placed. She could read nothing in the other's enigmatic gaze and after a moment Christian turned to her brother, holding out her hand for aid. Immediately Campbell Frazer was on his feet, but she appeared not to see his outstretched hand and taking Craigraven's arm limped slowly from the room.

'I hope your stay with us will be happy,' said the factor surprisingly into the silence.

Caro regarded him thoughtfully, wondering if he could possibly be unaware of the fact that she had been brought to the tower by force.

'As happy as possible—under the circumstances,' he added, reading her expression. Coming closer he added, confidentially, 'Please believe me, Miss Candover, while Craigraven has my loyalty, I do not condone his action . . . If I can be of any assistance, do pray call upon me.'

There was the slightest emphasis upon the

'any' and Caro's heart beat faster at the possible prospect of an unexpected ally, lifting one eyebrow she regarded him with an unspoken question in her dark eyes. She thought he returned her gaze significantly, but before she could do more than wonder, Craigraven returned and the factor turned away abruptly, seeming to confirm her suspicions with his haste.

It was with unusual docility that she allowed the tall Scotsman to lead her to her room, her mind busy with the possible use to which his factor might be put. Listening intently as Alan MacKenzie closed the door upon her, she felt a rush of excitement as no sounds of key turning or bolt barring carried through the thick wood. With a growing sense of anticipation she sat down to wait until the stronghold slept.

CHAPTER
FIVE

SITTING on her bed Caro fought the waves of sleep which threatened to overwhelm her. The stub of candle which had lighted her to the tiny room had long since guttered into a pool of melted wax and the dim moon that crept in at the narrow windows was the only source of illumination. Slowly the tower settled itself to rest and gradually the sounds made by its inmates faded into deep silence. At last the English girl stirred and rose stiffly to her feet, drawing the plaid Craigraven had given her about her shoulders before creeping quietly to the door.

Cautiously she opened it, the iron latch cold and heavy under her shaking hand as she paused on the threshold, her ears straining for any sound. None came and she moved carefully forward, her eyes trying to pierce the thick darkness that met her. She had hoped that a candle might have been left burning but all was in blackness, the pale, watery moonlight from the windows behind her merely showing the inky well of the stairs which descended at her feet.

Clutching her resolution about her like a comforting blanket, Caro began to descend cautiously, her feet reaching for each step. One hand on the cold stone wall and the other feeling ahead she went down until the stairs ended and she knew that she must cross the hall where they had spent the evening. The door was ajar and holding her breath she slipped through the slight gap, tense with apprehension.

Barely-discerned furniture huddled in unfamiliar shapes, the long windows pale ghosts in the velvet blackness. Her ears pricked for any sound Caro paused, searching the dark room until she felt safe to move. With hands outstretched before her, feeling like Lady Macbeth in the sleep-walking scene, she edged forward, hoping she remembered the position of the door in the far wall.

Nearly half-way across the black void, she came into sudden contact with a spindly card table and before she could save herself had pitched headlong, bringing the table down with a clatter which shattered the silence. Completely disorientated she tried to free herself from the embrace of fragile wooden legs and in the process realised that a pain was stinging the palm of her hand.

Suddenly she became aware of movement at the fireplace and a shaft of light pierced the darkness pinning her like a moth against a board.

'Going somewhere, Miss Candover?' asked Craigraven, rising from a deep chair.

Slowly, deliberately he walked across to tower over her as she lay on the floor. Blinking as the beam from the lantern was played on her face, Caro put up a hand to shade her eyes, and wished desperately that she was not in such an undignified position. The table was across her body, one foot was through a tear in her petticoat and she was unhappily aware that she was showing an inordinate amount of stockinged leg.

Having gazed at her for an uncomfortable length of time, Alan MacKenzie bent and tossed aside the card table allowing her to sit up and extricate her foot from the torn frill. With her head bent she took longer about the task than was necessary and growing impatient the Scotsman put both hands about her waist and hoisted her to her feet like a doll.

Hanging in his hands, Caro put a hand on his arm to steady herself and finding her fingers wet, looked down to see a black glistening stain smeared across her palm.

'I fear I have broken one of your glasses,' she said, almost conversationally.

'You have not answered my question,' Craigraven said unpleasantly, ignoring her remark.

'I was hoping you'd forgotten to lock your front door,' she told him ingenuously.

There was a pause while her captor digested this and then her honesty was rewarded by a bark of laughter. 'I begin to like you, Miss Candover,' he said, shaking her slightly.

'And I am beginning to bleed over your coat.'

'Ah, now I understand your remark about my glasses,' said Alan MacKenzie looking down at the welling blood. Leaving her, he crossed to the fire and blowing an ember into life, lit first a taper and then a candle. 'Come to the light,' he commanded, 'and let me look at your hand.'

'It's nothing—I can manage.'

'Do as I say, woman—I'll not have you bleeding over my floor, as well as my coat.'

Reluctantly Caro obeyed him, unwilling to allow him to minister to her. Taking her hand in his he held it to the light, gently probing with one finger. Involuntarily she winced and drew back.

'There is glass in the wound. I must hurt you a little more.'

Spreading her fingers, he bent over her hand, his fingers busy with the gaping cut across her palm. A strange emotion, compounded of pain and something like pleasure at his touch, startled the English girl and she stared down at his bent head with wide eyes. As if aware of her scrutiny Craigraven turned to meet her gaze momentarily before, taking a handkerchief from his pocket, he bound her hand and gravely returned it to her.

'Th-thank you,' said Caro, her voice shaking with the unexpected emotion that filled her, and reluctant to end the strange interlude, she sought for means of prolonging it. 'W-were you waiting for me?' she asked.

'By now, Miss Candover, I am well aware that I have taken no meek and mild prisoner. I thought you might have some such escapade in mind.'

Caroline studied his face. 'Why then did you not lock me in?' she asked.

'I wanted to see if you had the womanly capacity of breaking your word,' he told her with grim amusement.

Caro's gaze fell and taking pity on the

forlorn figure before him, Craigraven took her elbow and led her to the chair he had lately vacated.

'Sit,' he said, 'and take a glass of wine with me—if you have left any intact, that is.'

While he found and filled two glasses, she stared into the dying fire, fiddling with the rough bandage on her hand. So deep in thought was she that Craigraven's offer of the glass startled her, making her stare up at him, her eyes dark shadows in the flickering light.

'Is the cut bothering you?'

She shook her head and taking the glass from him, murmured her thanks before she sipped.

The Scotsman took up a stance in front of the enormous fireplace, leaning his arm along the long mantelpiece as he watched his captive above the rim of his glass. Well aware of his gaze Caro bore it as long as she could before, raising her chin, she returned his glance with a hint of questioning defiance in her eyes.

'Why do you want me to stay?' she asked. 'I would have thought you would have preferred to imprison me in your deepest dungeon rather than to drink and converse with me.'

He smiled faintly, and one eyebrow

arched. 'Which would you prefer, Miss Candover?'

Caro twisted the stem of the glass, watching the swirling liquid. 'I—must confess that I have very little liking for damp, dark places,' she admitted, realising almost at once her tactical mistake in supplying him with such knowledge. 'Though it does seem somewhat late for a *tête-à-tête*,' she added hastily, hoping to divert his attention from her previous statement.

'Not very flattering, Miss Candover— soon I shall begin to believe you have no liking for my company.'

'Liking or no, I seem to have no choice.'

There was a pause and wondering if she had gone too far in her plain speaking, Caro stole a glance at the silent Scotsman, to find him regarding her sombrely.

'I would by far prefer to treat you as an honoured guest in my house,' Craigraven said gravely. 'I must remind you that you gave me your word not to attempt to escape—'

'I discount a promise made under duress,' Caro told him loftily.

'Then, I am afraid that I have no choice other than to treat you as a prisoner. I see you have finished your wine—come, I will escort you back to your room.'

Feeling that she had acted churlishly in refusing the opportunity presented to her, the English girl set down her glass and rose to her feet. Craigraven was a silent presence at her elbow as she climbed the twisting stairs to her turret prison and bidding her a curt 'goodnight', he closed the heavy door behind her. A key grated in the lock and with a shudder of distaste Caro realised that she was in truth a captive in the little round chamber.

She was awoken by the sound of the door opening and realised, as Morag entered bearing a tray and water jug, that she had slept soundly, despite the alarms and excitement of the previous night.

'Here's hot water for your toilet and porridge for your breakfast,' the housekeeper announced, setting her burden down on the table. 'And when you're ready, Miss Christian says she'll be in the garden, if you've a mind to take a breath of air.'

Before Caro could express her surprise, the older woman whisked out of the room with a swirl of petticoats. Curious that Craigraven's sister should have issued such an invitation, Caroline washed and ate her breakfast quickly, eager to learn the reason for the apparent overture of friendship.

Trying the door she found it unlocked and ran down the stairs, across the hall, where the only sign of her nocturnal escapade was a dark stain on a newly-washed rug, and down the remaining twisting flight of narrow steps to the ground floor.

The main door stood open, a flood of sunlight pouring in to highlight the crisscrossed ironwork of the yett which could be barred behind the door to doubly safeguard the entrance. For a moment she paused regarding the anachronism of which, until then, she had only heard in tales of knights and ancient battles. Struck by the different world she had entered she touched the cold iron bars with one finger, before walking out of the tower and into the waiting sunshine.

Warmth struck her as she left the stone building and looking up she saw that the sky was a luminous, cloudless blue against which the tall walls of Craigraven Tower stood out, a brilliant, sparkling white as if newly-washed. Shading her dazzled eyes, she looked across to where the garden gate stood invitingly open and picking up her skirts made her way over the cobbled yard.

'Come in, Miss Candover,' came a gentle command as she hesitated in the gateway and following the voice, Caro saw that the

Scots girl was seated nearby, gazing expectantly at her.

'Thank you for letting me share your garden,' Caro said impulsively, gazing round at the neat little box hedges that protected the more delicate plants, at the flowering shrubs and spring bulbs nodding their colourful heads. Fruit trees were trained to grow against the ancient walls, and two bushes cut into peacocks guarded the stone seat on which Christian MacKenzie sat.

She seemed pleased with Caro's remark. 'My mother began it when she came here as a bride,' she said.

'And do you have green fingers?'

'*Green* fingers?' Christian repeated, obviously puzzled by the expression.

'We say that someone good at gardening has green fingers,' the English girl explained.

Laughing, Craigraven's sister held out her hands for inspection. 'I enjoy being busy in my garden, but my fingers remain the usual colour—if a wee bit dirty.'

'I'm surprised that so much grows here,' Caro went on, looking about. 'It seems so cold and bleak—'

The other shook her head. 'Not always,' she said. 'Just about now we are due for the peat weather, when folk away to the hills to cut peats for the winter. We should have about three weeks' fine weather—long enough to do all the work.'

'Today is lovely, just right for a walk or a ride—' Dismayed at her lack of tact, Caro broke off and gazed contritely at the seated girl. 'I'm sorry,' she said awkwardly, 'but I do not know precisely how you are placed. 'D-do you walk—or ride at all?'

'Ride, no. Walk—a little.'

Caro hesitated, then: 'W-would you like a turn about the garden?' she asked. 'I have a very strong arm and would be only too pleased to lend it to you.'

Christian MacKenzie looked steadily up at her, her expression considering, before her face relaxed. 'That would be pleasant,' she smiled, holding out her hand. Looking down at Caroline's hand as she leaned on her arm, she lightly touched the bandage covering the English girl's palm.

'Alan tells me that you are given to sleepwalking,' she commented, a teasing note in her voice.

'Not very successfully,' replied her companion.

'I hope you did not hurt yourself badly.'

'Mainly my dignity. Your brother can be very intimidating, especially when one is rolling round at his feet, imprisoned in one's own petticoats and wrestling with the legs of a table!'

This time Christian put back her head and laughed aloud. Looking up at her, for like her brother she was tall, Caroline was pleased to see the lines of strain in her face relax slightly and a tinge of colour creep into the pale cheeks. Why, she thought, surprised by the knowledge, we could be friends, and reading the other's eyes knew that the Scots girl felt the same affinity. With a smile and a nod the realisation was acknowledged silently and they continued their walk along the grass paths.

They strolled until Christian grew tired and then sat on the stone seat and talked, eager to get to know one another. In midsentence, Caro became uneasy and, suddenly aware of being watched, turned quickly to see that Craigraven and his factor had entered the garden.

Although he bowed gallantly and began a pleasant conversation, Caro was uneasily aware that his arrival was not due merely to a wish for female company. After a while she knew that her suspicions were well founded; with a bow he proffered his arm, commenting that he proposed to take her on a tour of inspection of the tower.

'I have promised to show Miss Caro some

of my embroidery,' put in Christian, endeavouring to come to her rescue.

'Later will do—there is plenty of time.'

'I need some help to—'

'Campbell here, has a strong right arm at your service,' Craigraven told her, holding her eye in a steady gaze until she frowned and looked away. Turning back to the English girl, he again crooked his elbow and reluctantly she put her fingers on his velvet sleeve. His hand closed over hers in the approved fashion, the tingle of excitement given by his touch astonishing her as it had the previous night.

'Is there much of the tower to see?' she asked as they left the garden. 'I thought I had seen most of it.'

'Och, yes—there's still a fair bit you haven't seen,' she was told blandly as they entered the cool, dim building.

She had expected to climb the stairs, supposing that it was the battlements she was to view, but instead they passed the narrow staircase and Craigraven unlatched a low door behind the rising steps. A dank, musty smell rose to meet them and Caro involuntarily stepped back.

'No—I'd rather not—!' she exclaimed, but suddenly the fingers resting on hers tightened their grip and Craigraven pressed her hand against his side, holding her prisoner.

Silently Jock MacKenzie appeared behind them, a lighted lantern in his hand, which he gave to his master, before retiring as quietly as he had come.

'I'm sure you will be interested,' the tall man assured the girl by his side, drawing her forward towards the brink of the dark opening.

'I will not,' Caro told him positively digging in her heels. 'I have no wish whatsoever to visit your cellars.'

'I can always carry you, Miss Candover.'

Lifting her head Caro studied the face above, searching for some softening in the cold gaze. 'I—know why you want me to go down there,' she told him.

He raised an eyebrow, 'Indeed?'

'Yes. I was foolish enough to let you know I am afraid of such places—and you are threatening to shut me d-down there.'

A hard smile crossed his face. 'Precisely so,' he agreed.

'Then, there is no need actually to go is there?' Caro pointed out, an unconscious hint of pleading in her voice.

'Now there, Miss Candover, you are mistaken. I think it a very good thing if you know exactly what faces you if you do not do what I want.'

And with the words, as if growing impatient, Craigraven slid his grip down her arm to her wrist and began to descend the stairs, dragging her after him with scant regard for her struggles or protests.

'The steps are narrow and worn,' he pointed out, his voice echoing in the enclosed space. 'If you should fall, I fear you would come to some hurt.'

Pride came to the English girl's aid and stifling her fears, she forced herself to follow her captor.

The lantern sent grotesque black shadows dancing ahead of them and putting her free hand against the wall to steady herself, she brought it away wet with moisture that oozed from the dank stones. After an age they reached the floor and Craigraven held the lantern aloft, letting its dim rays play on their surroundings. The light did not penetrate to the far corners, but Caro could see that a mouldering door faced them, its thick planks eaten by age and rodents, the iron grille above the huge bolt thick with rust.

'In a more savage age, Miss Candover, our prisoners were held here,' the Scotsman told her almost conversationally. 'And that round grille in the floor covers the oubliette— a deep well-like hole, where the most recalcitrant captives were kept.'

Caro closed her eyes at the horrid vision conjured up by his words, feeling a cold perspiration break out on her forehead as a deathly sickness threatened to engulf her. A deep shudder shook her and feeling her wrist tremble in his grasp Craigraven turned to look down at his captive.

Her frightened eyes were deep hollows in her white face, making her resemble one of the long-forgotten prisoners. Slowly her shaking hand reached towards him and clutched his sleeve.

'Don't—please don't—' she whispered, her voice a rustle of dry leaves. Her head bent and like a frightened child, she hid her face against his chest.

For a second Craigraven was still, an unfathomable expression in his grey eyes before, releasing her wrist, he put his arm round her drooping form. Forgetting the circumstances and grateful for the comfort of his touch, Caro leaned her weight against him. Waiting until she had recovered somewhat the Scotsman gently put her away, a supporting hand under her elbow.

'Let us go upstairs,' he said, quietly, leading her up the worn steps.

Gradually the lighter oblong of the door drew nearer, until at last Caro could step out into the hall by the main door. Weak with relief, she hurried to the doorway and leaned against the wall, breathing deeply and filling her eyes with the open space outside the tower.

'We have work to do,' Craigraven reminded her, his hand urging her towards the staircase.

Leaving the outer world reluctantly Caro walked ahead of the tall Scot up the winding stairs pausing, with a questioning glance, in the great hall.

'This will do, Miss Candover,' Craigraven agreed, pulling out a chair. 'Pray seat yourself.'

Obeying him, Caro watched as paper and ink were set before her. Taking a knife from his pocket, her companion cut a new quill into a point and placed it beside the paper. With one hand resting on the table the Scotsman leaned over her, his steady gaze holding hers until her eyes wavered and fell.

'I think we will have no argument,' he said, significantly, and she made no pretence of not understanding his meaning. 'You will write a letter to the Governor of Inverness—'

Caro clasped her hands together under cover of the table and stared down at the thick paper.

'Or,' Craigraven went on inexorably, 'we shall be forced to change your lodgings.'

'Why don't you just say that you will shut me in your dungeon?' she demanded, her voice high.

'Is there any need?' he asked, his tone deceptively gentle and she was forced to concede silently that there was not.

Wordlessly she reached out, pulling the paper nearer and dipped the pen into the black ink. As she hesitated over the heading, Craigraven settled himself on the table beside her, one long leg swinging.

'Begin by addressing your father,' he advised easily. 'I have no wish for him to know your whereabouts.'

The quill scratched and spluttered across the page, the writing shaking with her nervousness. The Scotsman watched the forming words.

'"General Candover, the Governor, Inverness. Honoured Sir",' he read, a frown forming between his eyebrows. 'Rather formal, Miss Candover,' he remarked.

Caro raised her eyes briefly. 'He will know my writing,' she told him briefly, pen poised. 'What shall I say?'

'Merely that you are captive and to obtain your return, he must release all political prisoners in his keeping—use your own words, but for your own sake, I would advise you to use your best powers of persuasion.'

Caro brushed her lips with the tip of the quill feather and after a few seconds' thought began to write busily, handing it silently to the waiting man when she had finished.

'Very succinct,' he said, having perused it, 'if a trifle ill-formed, but doubtless signs of agitation in your writing will serve as a goad to a fond father—I trust he is a fond parent?'

'Oh, yes,' the English girl agreed, enigmatically. 'Very fond.'

'I am glad to hear it.'

Rising, Caro wandered across to the window embrasure. 'What if he should decide that he will not be intimidated—that I am not to be exchanged?' she asked, trying to sound casual, while waves of apprehension sent icy fingers down her spine.

'My dear Miss Candover, do not, I pray, dwell upon that possibility.'

The silky voice made her swing round to find the speaker much nearer than she had anticipated; he had left the table and was standing behind her, one hand on the wall above her head, effectively imprisoning her in the deep window.

'There are ways of making a fond father amenable to an abductor's demands,' he told her, his tone full of quiet menace.

Her eyes wide and blank with fear, Caro's hand crept to her mouth as she backed away until brought up by the window at her back.

'If you so wish, feel free to add a rider to your letter. Perhaps a plea will touch your father's heart. It would be a shame if all should be lost for want of a little endeavour.'

With a calculating smile, he stepped back leaving the way clear and Caro brushed past him, hurrying to the writing-table in a flurry of skirts. Quickly she scribbled a few more lines, before flinging the pen away, she averted her head, ashamed of the fear Craigraven had produced in her.

'"Pray do not fail me—I am afraid for my life".' Craigraven read aloud, not hiding the satisfaction the addition afforded him. 'Very good, Miss Candover, *exactly* what I wanted.'

Caroline sat up. 'You did it deliberately!' she accused, her eyes blazing in her white face. 'Y-you deliberately set out to frighten me—to make me think—' To her horror she burst into tears and hid her face in her hands as violent sobs shook her.

'Better that, my lassie, than the real thing. If your postscript does the trick, you have nothing more to fear.'

Wiping her wet cheeks with the palms of her hands, Caro glared at him, heedless of the wild appearance she presented. 'I hate you—oh, *how* I hate you!' she cried, shaking with the aftermath of fear and rage.

Dropping a handkerchief into her lap, Craigraven turned away indifferently. 'As you wish,' he said, shrugging, as he scattered sand over her letter to dry the ink, before folding and sealing it.

'You are a brigand, a bandit—an uncivilised savage, no better than the Red Indians in the Americas! You puffed-up peacock, tartan trickster—'

He eyed her dispassionately. 'You, my fine English lady, remind me of a fish wife from Aberdeen,' he told her coldly cutting across her rush of words, and turning on his heel, left the room.

CHAPTER
SIX

LEFT alone Caroline sobbed unrestrainedly for a few moments, her head pillowed on her arms before growing calmer, she blew her nose, wiped her eyes and sat up.

'Come away to my room and I'll make us a wee cuppie,' came a soft voice and Craigraven's sister touched her shoulder. 'Isn't he the brute, just?'

Caro raised her tearstained face. 'You heard?'

'Some of it,' Christian paused awkwardly, 'He's not so fierce really. It's just that he's worried over Rory. He's our young brother you know, and Alan has had a care for him since he was a wee laddie himself.'

She put out her hand invitingly and putting her own into it the English girl accompanied her from the great hall, up the familiar flight of stairs past her own little round chamber and into one of the rooms leading off the tiny landing.

Christian's room was different from any

that Caro had seen at the tower. About a quarter the size of the hall below, it was well-proportioned and furnished comfortably to fulfil all the Scots girl's needs. A four-poster bed stood against the wall furthest from the fireplace, two chairs and a table stood in front of the small fire, over which a little copper kettle steamed gently. Two long windows let in a good amount of light while on one cushioned window-seat lay some discarded embroidery and near the other a small bookshelf held several volumes.

'What a pleasant room!' Caro exclaimed, surprised to find such a different atmosphere from the rest of the castle. 'How comfortable you must be.'

The other girl smiled and busied herself with making the tea, not speaking until they were both settled with shallow cups in their hands, aromatic steam rising from the golden liquid.

'Alan feels responsible for Rory, you see,' she began after a while. 'The eldest stays at home to keep the estate safe and the other sons fight for the cause—it's always arranged so.'

'Very sensible,' her companion agreed.

Christian looked up sharply at the dry tone. 'It doesn't mean that we care the less,' she said, 'though in this instance I do not believe that Craigraven would have offered the Prince his sword, Scotland has his loyalty.'

'That I can believe,' Caro admitted feelingly.

'You mustn't think him hard or cruel—'

'He has been both to me!'

'He does what he feels is right—and to rescue Rory is *right*! We cannot leave him in the Bridge Hole to rot or be transported—or worse. You can't expect us not to do our utmost to save him. We'd do anything—' She faltered under the other's steady gaze.

'I have good cause to believe you,' Caro said, quietly. 'And am only sorry that I have been caught up in your machinations.' Biting her lip, she stared blankly ahead fighting for self-control as she crossed her arms and hugged herself. 'God, I was *so* afraid!' she burst out suddenly. 'It makes me ashamed to know that I could be frightened so much by another human being! I'm not an animal or a child and yet I . . . would have done anything he asked at that moment. I—disgust myself!'

'Oh, Caro—don't be so hard on yourself. Alan set out to frighten you into doing what he wanted. At times I'm afraid of him and I'm his sister. He can be very intimidating.'

The English girl looked at the other. 'He seems kind enough to you.'

'Usually—but there are times—' she broke off and looked down at the cup in her hands. 'He wants me to marry Campbell Frazer and I know he won't let me prevaricate for much longer.'

'And you don't want to?'

The bowed, fair head was shaken silently and Caro eyed her companion thoughtfully. 'May I know why?' she asked. 'He seems very suitable.'

'There are . . . reasons. I do not trust him. Alan thinks he's a friend, but I'm not so sure.'

She seemed about to say more, but caught herself up and closed her mouth over whatever she had been about to say, instead taking Caro's cup to refill it, determinedly beginning an artless conversation as she did so.

Accepting her lead, Caroline answered automatically, thinking of the half-spoken suspicions and wondering if they could be used to her own advantage; if the factor was not entirely Craigraven's man, then perhaps he could be persuaded to aid her? Determined to give the matter her attention as soon as possible she put the subject aside for the moment and set herself out to win Christian MacKenzie's confidence and friendship.

In all truth she found this no difficult thing to accomplish; the Scots girl was lonely and almost pathetically eager for a friend, while to her surprise Caro found that even under such inauspicious circumstances, she liked Craigraven's sister and that an affinity appeared ready to grow between them even without her efforts.

'What happened to you?' she asked a little later, 'I know you had a fall from a horse . . . Pray don't think me merely nosey or inquisitive. No one mentions it and it can't be good for you to keep it buried.' She paused shyly and looked away before adding: 'I would help if I could.'

Christian did not answer at once and Caro wondered uneasily if she had hurt or upset the other girl with her question.

'I—do not talk about it because no one believes me when I do,' the Scots girl said at last. 'They all think the accident has knocked me silly—or that I am making excuses for my own incompetence. But until it happened I was near as good a rider as my brother.'

'Tell me,' Caro said simply.

'I took Alan's great gelding, something I admit I should not have done, but I had done it before and he was none the wiser. The minute I mounted him I knew something was wrong, he took off—behaved like a maniac, bucking until he threw me. As I lay there, half-unconscious with pain and fright someone came and took something from under the saddle—then Alan arrived and the others . . .' Her voice trailed off.

'You think someone put something under the saddle?'

Christian nodded briefly. 'A thistlehead would have that effect and be easily found.'

'But why—and who?'

Christian shrugged her thin shoulders and looked away, but Caro had the feeling that the other girl could have spoken a name if she had wished.

'And you've no idea who came?' she asked.

'No—my head was swimming and I was near unconscious.'

'But you suspect someone, don't you?'

Christian remained silent, her blue gaze steady. 'I'll tell you one day,' she pronounced and the English girl knew that she had not yet passed the final test of friendship and abandoned the puzzling subject for the moment.

'If this was almost a year ago, surely you should be better now?' she asked.

'Craigraven says I do not take enough exercise to make my leg strong again. He is right—but, you see, when I am well again he has promised Campbell Frazer that we shall marry.'

'Surely he would not make you wed against your will?' said Caro, shocked.

'It would be a suitable marriage. You said so yourself—but I do not care for him.'

'Then tell your brother so!'

Christian laughed bitterly. 'Haven't I just, and himself not listening, only saying that liking will come once we're wed. Oh, he's a brute at times!'

The English girl sent her a speaking glance and they both smiled.

'I'll miss you when you've gone,' Christian said involuntarily.

Caro controlled the shiver of dread that slipped down her back like an icy raindrop and asked casually, 'Who went with the message—w-will it take long?'

'Johnnie, Alan's foster brother went with it. He should be back in a week—ten days at the most.'

Caroline looked out of the window, breathing on a pane and drawing a face with her finger. Apparently intent upon her handiwork, she asked, 'What will happen if the Governor won't do as Craigraven asks?'

'Of course he will,' cried the Scottish girl, in tones that proved she had never considered such a possibility. 'No father would hesitate under the circumstances.'

'His loyalty to his commission might prove stronger than his affection,' Caro told her evenly. 'And then what, Christian. What would Craigraven do then?'

The other girl had been unable to answer and Caro put the same question to Alan MacKenzie himself later the same day. The weather had been fine and the inhabitants of the tower house had taken themselves into the garden after dinner. By careful arrangement which she could not but admire, the factor had contrived to accompany Christian, leaving the master of Craigraven to walk beside his prisoner.

'We'll think about that if and when the need arises,' he told her, appearing uninterested.

'You must have already given the matter thought,' she pointed out. 'And as the principal involved I would like to know what possible fate you have in store for me.'

Alan MacKenzie broke step, turning to look down at her challenging face. 'Will you be any happier to know?' he queried.

'Perhaps not—but I like to know what to expect. Surprises are only enjoyable if they are pleasant. I do not really care for the unexpected.'

'Sometimes, Miss Candover, it is better not to know what is ahead—' He broke off and shook his head at her as she caught her breath at his words. 'Neither, Miss Candover, is it a good thing to read more into my words than is said. I merely meant that often if one knew what lay ahead, then the present would be spoiled. As it is at this moment the weather and setting are both pleasant, let us enjoy them. Perhaps we could even contrive to find one another's company convivial. What do you say?'

Caro searched his face, her own gaze thoughtful. 'Perhaps,' she answered hesitantly.

'Just until Johnnie returns let us pretend that you are a friend of Christian's here on a visit. I shall be a host *par excellence* and you will be a guest happy to be among us.' Grey eyes smiled down into hers. 'Pax, Miss Candover?' he suggested, holding out his hand.

'Pax,' she agreed, putting her fingers into his, once again experiencing a tingle of pleasure at his touch. Surprised by her own reaction and disturbed by his presence, she broke away, ostensibly to examine a flowering shrub, but in reality to recover her composure.

'Would you care to ride tomorrow?'

Craigraven asked, surprising her by the hint of deference in his voice.

'Why, yes—I would, but what about your sister?'

'She has not ridden since her accident.'

Caro thought he had finished speaking, but after a short pause, he went on, 'I—think she *will not* rather than cannot . . . if she could be encouraged perhaps—'

For the first time they exchanged glances of mutual understanding and then Caro nodded.

'I'll see if there's anything I can do,' she promised, but when she approached Christian she found the other girl adamant.

'No!' she said decidedly, 'I have no wish to ride.'

Caro watched her hands twist together. 'Just come and see me mount,' she cajoled, thinking that to persuade the Scots girl to visit the stables would be a start. 'I'm used to riding side-saddle, but your brother tells me that Scottish ladies ride astride.'

Christian smiled. 'We do,' she agreed, 'but not when we wish to impress. In town we'd ride pillion—but in the hills it's safer to ride astride. You'll find it not very difficult. Alan will teach you.'

Caro was not sure whether she viewed the prospect of Craigraven's tutorship with apprehension or interest but, when the next day, she went to the stables after breakfast, it was to find the factor waiting for her.

'Craigraven finds he has other business,' he said, seeing her surprise at his presence.

Ashamed to realise that she felt chagrined at the tall Scot's absence, Caroline smiled her brightest and allowed the factor to help her on to the little garron's back. Once there she found that her full skirt fell about her in folds, hiding her legs more respectably than she had supposed possible. It felt strange to place her feet in the very long stirrups either side of the sturdy animal's body, but on the whole she was reasonably comfortable and felt some of her qualms evaporate as they trotted out of the courtyard gate.

It was the first time she had been outside the castle since they had arrived and while her imprisonment had hardly been arduous, she felt a surge of pleasure as they left the buildings behind and headed towards the surrounding mountains. The track was rough and ill-defined, but the tiny garron picked his way with ease and the English girl, seated on the goatskin which served as a saddle, felt safe enough to relax and gaze about.

They were climbing steadily and looking back, she could see Craigraven Tower, like a white sentinel perched on its rocky outcrop. Following her gaze Frazer Campbell drew rein, staring at the castle himself, with an expression Caro could not define.

'The situation is well chosen,' he said almost speaking to himself. 'It guards the meeting place of the mountain passes and yet is remote enough to be almost secret.'

Caroline looked at him reflectively. 'Have you lived here long?' she asked.

'My mother was sister to Craigraven's mother,' he told her briefly as if all was answered. 'I was brought up to be his second hand, his trusty servant.'

The hint of bitterness in his tone made her glance quickly at him, but his face told her nothing.

'The tower has been your home?'

'My mother and I were given refuge in return for our labour and loyalty. She was housekeeper until she died and I was brought up to be a general factotum, some-one whose loyalty to the Craigraven family is beyond question.'

Caro felt an urge to ask if it was truly so, but after consideration decided to feel her way cautiously in case she was misjudging his attitude towards Alan MacKenzie; after all Frazer Campbell had not actually said anything to imply that his loyalty was other than solid, and her feelings that he disliked his position in the hierarchy of the tower could be wrong.

They rode on for a while until dark clouds appeared over the encircling hills and even though they turned back at once, a heavy downpour caught them before they reached the shelter of the castle.

Soaked and shivering the English girl slipped from the back of her mount and leaving the factor to see to the horses ran towards the tower, her head lowered against the driving rain. Not looking where she was going, the plaid clutched over her hair, she raced up the steps and through the front door, heading for the stairs, but before she reached them she hurtled against someone and would have fallen had not strong arms held her.

The door closed behind her and she was alone in the dark, held prisoner against a masculine chest. A strong heart beat rhythmically in her ear and the lace edging of a cravat tickled her nose. Despite the darkness she had a very good idea who it was embracing her and was not surprised when a familiar voice spoke above her head.

'Now who can this cold, wet little bundle be?' asked Craigraven, his voice soft and speculative.

Some perverse reason kept Caro silent and after a moment while one arm still clasped her securely, the other hand was raised to explore her face. Fingers lightly touched her cheek, outlined her eyebrows, smoothed her lips and slipped caressingly down her throat, lingering in the hollow at the base of her neck.

Stirring in his arms, she started back before his hand could venture further, only to be pulled closer and her struggles subdued until she was passive in the circle of his arm. The plaid had fallen to the floor and her wet clothes clung to her body in cold clammy folds. A violent shiver shook her, but whether from chill or excitement she could not tell.

A hand brushed her wet hair and down her damp shoulder. 'If you're not warmed soon, my hen, you'll die of cold,' Alan MacKenzie whispered, 'come away to my room and I'll make you forget the cold.' Feeling her resistance, he took her chin and tipped up her face. 'Who is it?' he asked, 'Jennie from the kitchen, or Mary who looks after the linen?'

When she did not answer, he bent closer in the darkness until his mouth found hers. His kiss was lingering, gentle as a butterfly's wing as he explored her lips, becoming deeper and more demanding until Caro's own response surprised her. Creeping up of their own volition, her hands clasped about Craigraven's neck, drawing his head down to hers. She returned his kisses with an enthusiasm that astonished her, but when his grasp became more insistent, urging her towards the stairs, she became aware of her danger and breaking away with a suddenness that surprised him, found the staircase by good luck and made her escape, scurrying up the treads like a panic stricken mouse.

Arriving at the top, she met Christian who had come to the stairhead to see what had caused her fright.

'They *are* rather dark,' she remarked, sympathetically taking it for granted that the lack of light was the source of Caroline's precipitous arrival and taking the English girl's arm, exclaimed upon her state of wetness and led her up to her room to change.

When they returned to the great hall, it was to find, Craigraven warming himself in front of the huge fireplace. Acutely conscious of his presence and the fact that they had lately been in such close physical contact, Caro avoided his eyes, but when he directed a question to her, she was forced to meet his gaze.

'Did you enjoy your ride, Miss Candover?'

'The poor wee thing was soaked to the skin and you have no idea of the fright she was in when I met her at the top of the stairs,' said Christian before the English girl could reply.

Craigraven's eyebrows rose. 'Really?' he queried. 'Now what, I wonder, could have caused that?' His voice was bland.

'Why that nasty, dark staircase, of course. Time and again I've told you that I've had a fright while climbing them. I'm sure a ghostie bides there.'

Alan MacKenzie turned his gaze on Caro. 'And you, Miss Candover, what have you to say?'

Caroline eyed him, her colour rising as she recognised the Scot's self-satisfied teasing. 'About this nasty presence on the stairs?' she asked, glowering at him along the length of her nose. 'I'd certainly say there was something decidedly unpleasant there when I came up!'

'Strange—I followed you and yet I did not hear you call out, but then I've often heard that you females enjoy such encounters.'

'Well, a lantern set against the wall would solve our problems,' put in his sister, unaware of the by-play between her two companions.

'What say you, Miss Candover—would a

light solve the problems of the staircase?'

For the first time a glimmer of amusement showed in her eyes. 'I think it might add to them,' she could not resist saying.

An answering gleam appeared in Craigraven's grey gaze. 'You think some mysteries are better left in the dark?'

'I think there are some answers that could be embarrassing!' she retorted.

'What are you two talking about?' complained his sister, 'I don't understand a word you are saying.'

'Forgive me, Christian,' Alan MacKenzie said at once and turned to bow in Caro's direction. 'And I must beg your pardon Miss Candover.'

She raised her eyebrows, 'For what, sir?' she asked, her eyes daring him to answer.

'For allowing you to be frightened on the stairs—in future you have only to ask and I shall have pleasure in accompanying you whenever you use them.'

'My thanks,' Caro returned, having digested this, 'but I have no fear of ghosts. I am quite capable of dealing with whatever I might find there.' She paused a moment and then asked delicately. 'Pray sir, how is your arm? I trust the wound is healing well . . . I fancied that you favoured your shoulder a little.'

'I thank you for your enquiries,' the tall Scot answered gravely. 'Until you spoke I had forgot about it.'

The English girl smiled, 'I rather thought you had,' she remarked enigmatically and was pleased to see that her shaft had struck home.

Before she could move away Craigraven had taken her hand and turned it palm up to inspect the neat bandage. 'And your wound is as well as mine, I trust?'

In fact it was paining her, but having no intention of telling him that Caroline assured him that all was well and determinedly withdrew her hand. Later on, however, she told Christian the truth and they inspected the angry, swollen gash together.

'Morag should see this,' decided the Scots girl. 'She's a great one for treating sores and ills. Alan says that in a less enlightened age she would have been burned as a witch.'

'Tch, tch,' muttered the housekeeper when she saw the inflamed cut. 'What a silly lassie you are, why did you no show it me before?'

'It didn't seem too bad until today, I think holding the reins must have aggravated it.'

Morag sent her a searching look. 'And you came home wet to the skin, so I hear tell. That Campbell Frazer has no more sense than a flea! Doesn't he set out to cause trouble just.'

Caro pricked her ears at this confirmation of Christian's hinted suspicions. 'Don't you like him?' she asked casually.

'Like him, and him half a Campbell!'

The English girl blinked. 'Is that bad?'

'Bad! And him with the bold, bad, black heart of a treacherous Campbell. Only himself can see no bad in the man and that's because Craigraven believes him honest and loyal . . . I'm no saying he's not, you ken,' the housekeeper added inconsequentially after her outburst, 'it's just that he's a Campbell and Campbells are not to be trusted.'

'I—see,' said Caro, wondering if she did. 'You really have no reason to dislike the factor save the fact that he's a Campbell?'

'I'll say no more,' Morag said darkly, 'but Miss Christian and me—we're alike in our thoughts—and no without reason. Campbell Frazer is no a man to cross, so you'll not be after repeating my words—or anyone else's if you're wise. Accidents have a way of happening to folk who have displeased the factor.'

Digesting this interesting information Caro fell silent while the housekeeper bathed her hand. A sharp pain made her jerk her

hand back with an involuntary exclamation
as a swab gently cleansed the wound.

'What's to do?' inquired Craigraven from
the open doorway, where he had caught
sight of the operation. Coming into the room
he peered at Morag's task, before taking
Caro's hand in his, he examined the inflamed
cut.

'I'd say there was a wee bittee glass in it,'
the housekeeper said.

'I'm inclined to agree with you,' he
answered finding that even the gentlest of
touches made the English girl flinch. 'Come
to the window,' he commanded and still
holding her hand drew her across the room
and studied her palm in the better light.
Feeling her tremble slightly as he gently
probed, he sent her a fleeting glance. 'Sit on
the window-seat,' he advised briefly, before
returning to his task.

Obeying him, Caro watched his bent head
and knew a strange, almost overwhelming
urge to lift her free hand and touch the fair
hair so near to her. The sun streaming in at
the window struck gold and silver gleams
from each strand and she was intrigued by
the strength of each curling hair as it sprang
from his head before being smoothed back
and confined by the black silk bow at the
nape of his neck.

As if aware of her eyes, Craigraven looked up suddenly and she hastily lowered her gaze as he asked Morag for a needle. Taking his little black knife from its sheath, he carefully washed and wiped it and then leaned against the shutter while waiting for the housekeeper to supply his needs from her workbox.

'I'll do my best not to hurt you,' he promised, looking down at Caro.

'I'm not afraid,' she told him, finding to her surprise that she had confidence in the tall Scot. Nevertheless she had no liking for blood and quickly averted her head as he set to work to remove the sliver of glass, whose tip protruded from the puckered cut.

At last the ordeal was over, the wound cleansed and Craigraven wrapping a new dressing round her hand. Relief brought dizziness and the bright sun spun in dazzling circles making her close her eyes against the disagreeable sight.

An arm slipped round her shoulder and she was held firmly against the support of Craigraven's body. One hand smoothed her hair, while the Scot murmured soothingly.

'Now, now, my brave wee lassie—it's all over and done with. There's no more to bother about.'

Caro suffered his ministrations, finding

that she liked the unexpected attentions and long after the world had finished its gyrations she continued to lean against Craigraven's velvet jacket. Gradually his hand slid down until he was gently stroking first her cheek and then her neck, but when his fingers reached her shoulder and slipped beneath the edge of her lace fichu, she suppressed the shiver of excitement that the touch aroused and put up her good hand to detain his questing caress.

Alan MacKenzie's fingers twisted under her grasp and her hand was held in a firm grip as he seated himself beside her on the windowsill. Thoughtfully he looked down at her slim fingers and then unexpectedly, lifted her hand to his lips and gently kissed her curving palm. Raising his head he met her startled gaze and smiled into her eyes.

'For being a good girl, Miss Candover,' he explained. 'Did your mother never say that kisses are better than clouts?'

CHAPTER
SEVEN

FOR some time Caroline had suspected that she was attracted to her captor, who appeared not so formidable after all, but suddenly she found herself forced to admit that much deeper feelings were involved; it came to her one day with blinding clarity. She and Craigraven had been walking in the garden, when the tall Scot reached up and plucked a spray of cherry blossom which he presented to her with a gallant bow and as she looked into his smiling face, her heart gave a great bound.

Afraid he would read the emotion in her expression she looked down at the delicate white flowers in her hand and began to make inconsequential conversation, her manner deliberately light and gay. As soon as she could Caro ran ahead to join Christian who was ensconced on her favourite seat and, afraid of her own feelings, took care that the talk was general, avoiding any subject that was at all personal.

That night in bed, she lay awake wondering how her feelings towards Craigraven could have undergone such a change: only a short while before she hated the fair Scot and now . . . She shied away from the word 'love' and changing position in the crumpled bed tried to think of other matters, but her mind returned again and again to the forbidden subject. Alan MacKenzie was rude and overbearing, cruel and arrogant, ruthless to an astonishing degree, she told herself, but the image her mind called up was of an attentive, laughing man with a tender, teasing light in his grey eyes.

Bewildered and uneasy, nervous of her uncontrollable emotions, Caroline rose from her bed and went to the window, thinking that a glimpse of the dark, quiet night beyond the walls of Craigraven Tower might soothe her feelings, but when she knelt on the window-seat her attention was immediately attracted to a figure below. The fair hair of Alan MacKenzie was unmistakable as he leaned on the balustrade in the walled garden. He seemed lost in contemplation, but as the English girl watched, he lifted his head as if aware of her scrutiny.

As if spellbound Caro returned his gaze, a tiny pulse in her throat flickering, before he swept her a wide, elaborate bow and walked away. As soon as he was out of sight among the shadows, Caro ran across the room and leaping back into bed, pulled the covers up to her chin and lay there, eyes wide with anticipation. After a while when no sounds of approaching footsteps came to her straining ears, she relaxed and to her surprise, promptly fell asleep, for the next thing she knew was being awoken by the morning light.

A strange excitement possessed her all day; when Alan MacKenzie was near her, his very closeness seemed to charge the atmosphere with tension. So aware herself of each move he made and each word he spoke she was surprised that no one else seemed to notice the tension between them.

When dinner was served and the long day at last drawing to an end, Caro was unsure whether to be relieved or sorry. As usual the main course was mutton, cooked in the same unimaginative manner, which made the English girl look forward to the dessert, which was usually more appetising. A jelly and several fruit tarts had just been set on the table when a commotion below was heard. The sound of running feet on the stairs brought Craigraven to his feet, one hand on the hilt of his sword. The factor, too, rose quietly, pushing back his chair, while the two women gazed at each other, eyes dark with apprehension. Crossing the wide room quickly, Alan MacKenzie was beside the door as it opened, his big sword drawn and every muscle tense and ready for action.

Before entering Johnnie MacKenzie had the forethought to identify himself and by the time he had bounded in through the door, his master had relaxed and was in the process of sheathing his claymore.

'Craigraven, Craigraven!' the Highlander burst out and, his English deserting him in his stress, launched into a wild spate of Gaelic.

Only too well aware of the content of his speech Caroline watched Alan MacKenzie's face with growing apprehension. Rigid with disbelief he listened to his henchman, his features growing white with anger and when, with an abrupt gesture he stopped the smaller man and turned his gaze on the English girl, she drew back in dismay at the twin flames of fury dancing in his eyes.

Before she could do more than half-rise out of her seat, he had reached her. The flat of his hand hit the side of her face with such force that she was knocked from the chair to sprawl at his feet in an untidy heap of skirts and petticoats. Tears of pain blurred her vision as she put her hand to her stinging cheek, shocked by the unexpected violence. As she tried to gather her shaken wits, hands seized her upper arms in a cruel grip and she was dragged up to dangle helplessly, her toes barely touching the floor.

'So, Sassenach, you'd make a fool out of me!' snorted Craigraven, his face inches away from hers. 'Johnnie tells me they were dancing in the streets of Inverness to celebrate the wedding o' the Governor's daughter.'

With each word she was shaken back and forth until she thought her neck would break. Her teeth clanged together and her hair came loose from its confining pins and tumbled about her shoulders.

'Treacherous, conniving, lying—'

Winding her hand in the lace of his cravat she hung on grimly, tightening her grip until she had his attention.

'H-how can you name me so?' she demanded breathlessly, her head aching from his furious assault. '*You* were the one who thought me the Governor's daughter. *I* did not ask to be abducted.'

'And could ye no ha' told me?' he queried, his accent stronger than she had ever heard it. 'You led me on—letting me get fond of ye.'

'Fond?' she looked up at the word, but could see no fondness in his hard gaze as he stared down at her, his mouth grim in his furious face.

'What a fool you must have thought me, and how proud you must have been to wind Craigraven round your little finger!'

'Oh, no!' she whispered desperately, 'it wasn't like that.'

Beside himself with rage, looking ready for murder, he raised his hand to strike her again, but his arm was seized from behind.

'No, Alan,' cried Christian, holding on to his sleeve with all her strength. 'Alan, *Alan* would you have a Craigraven remembered for murdering a wench?'

As the words sank in, the Scotsman slowly lowered his arm and at last let Caroline go so abruptly that she had no chance to regain her balance and stumbled backwards until she tripped over the hem of her dress and sat down suddenly.

'What now, Craigraven?' asked Campbell Frazer and grateful for the interruption to draw attention away from herself the English girl stayed where she was while the room righted itself about her dizzy head.

'Oh, Alan, what of Rory?' asked Christian anxiously, and the glance she sent the other girl held none of its usual warmth.

'Trust me *mo ghoal*, and do not worry,' her brother told her using a Gaelic endearment from their childhood. 'Didn't I give you my word that Rory would be safe?'

'And the girl, Craigraven,' came Campbell's voice, 'what of her?'

A contemptuous grey glance was flung at Caro where she crouched, making her flush painfully. As the tall Scot walked towards her, it was all she could do not to flinch away and even so her quickened breathing made the lace at her breast rise and fall in agitation. The toe of a brogue stirred her, not ungently.

'On your feet, Miss Candover,' commanded Craigraven and offering her no aid, waited impassively while she scrambled up. 'What shall I do with you?' he wondered softly, his mouth cruel.

'I'd give you to my henchmen, but you're such a puny wee creature that you'd provide little sport for them . . . and if I sold you to a West Indian slave trader, the same would hold good—of course I *could* drop you down my oubliette and forget all about you.'

Her eyes opened wide in horror. 'You—wouldn't—' she whispered, her dry lips hardly moving and to her relief Craigraven shook his head.

'My sister's right—I have no wish to be

remembered as the MacKenzie who murdered a lassie—I'd much rather be talked of as the bold fellow who wedded the Sassenach woman.'

When the sense of his words sank in, Caro's eyes widened even further. 'Wedded!' she gasped.

Alan MacKenzie seemed pleased with her reaction. 'Why not?' he asked. 'A wife is a husband's chattel—married to me you'll no be able to give evidence against me and I'll be in my legal right to keep you under lock and key, if I wish.'

Shaken by his violent treatment and appalled by his suggestion Caroline drew herself up to her full height and facing Craigraven spoke out impulsively, 'I wouldn't marry you if the King himself wished it,' she said clearly, only the slight shake in her voice betraying the slender hold she had on her nervous fears.

'Will ye no, my fine lassie?' Alan MacKenzie asked silkily and as he moved towards her Caro wished fervently that she had controlled the anger that had made her defy him. 'Well, there you are wrong,' he went on deliberately, 'for if you'll no be wedded by a minister, then we'll be hand-fasted in the old Scots tradition and just to make sure, I bed with you before I leave.'

'Leave?' came Christian's anxious query and at once her brother turned to her.

'Dinna fuss yoursel', my hen,' he said, comfortingly. 'If I'm to save Rory then it stands to reason I must leave the tower, but you have my word that I will be back as soon as possible.'

For a moment the English girl was forgotten as brother and sister were united in a bond that struck a pang of envy in the other's heart, then the fair Scotsman turned back to her, his expression hardening perceptibly.

'Well, Sassenach, which is it to be?' he demanded, harshly. 'Do you wish to enjoy the benefits of the clergy—or shall we just away to your room?'

A shudder of distaste visibly shook her and her face was totally colourless. Disregarding her evident distress Craigraven deliberately looked her over, allowing his gaze to linger as it travelled slowly over her body.

'Make up your mind, miss, I've no time to spare . . . and to tell the truth I have a preference for the second proposition—that way I can put you aside when the need has passed.'

Caro swallowed with difficulty. 'I'll marry you,' she said tonelessly, knowing she had no other choice.

Craigraven nodded. 'Jock, away to fetch

the minister,' he commanded. 'And you, Campbell, take my intended bride to her room and lock her in.'

Shaking off the factor's arm, Caroline crossed to the door, exchanging speaking glances with Christian as she did so. Craigraven appeared not to notice the exchange, his attention already fully centred on the task of cleaning and priming the pistols taken from a wall cupboard.

Once within her room, the English girl listened to the key being turned in the lock of her prison, standing still until the sound of Campbell Frazer's retreating footsteps died away. A deep sigh escaped her and she made a fluttering gesture of hopelessness, before sinking down on the hard bed and covering her face with her hands. Her shoulders slumped in dejection she sat almost motionless for some hours, while her mind returned again and again to the miserable situation in which she found herself.

Strange as it now seemed, she had in fact almost forgotten the reason Craigraven and she found themselves in such close proximity; of course she had known that he must find out that she was not the Governor's daughter, but somehow she had been able to put the thought aside, disregarding it in the strange happiness she found in her captor's company, almost persuading herself that the deception did not matter—that Alan MacKenzie's feelings for her would continue even after he knew that his scheme had failed and that she was useless as an exchange for his brother.

Now reality had been brought home to her with cruel abruptness and it was clear that the fair Scot had no real affection for her; his kindness and tender gallantries had been no more than wiles to pass the time and gain her confidence. Hot tears scalded her cheeks and she let them fall unheeded, reflecting bitterly that while she had duped Craigraven he had fooled her more completely.

Time passed and although the hour was late the night was lit with the luminous quality with which Caroline had become familiar. Too despondent to look out of the window she had been aware of much activity both in, and outside the tower, as messengers were sent and others returned having completed their business. At last as the grey light began to leave the sky footsteps approached and holding her breath, she stood up, eyeing the door with apprehension.

'Come this way, mistress,' said Johnnie MacKenzie, avoiding her eye and reluctantly she obeyed.

When she entered the great hall, it was to find the other occupants of the tower already assembled there. Morag and Christian who were standing together looked up at her entrance but the factor and Craigraven who were talking to a thin man in black went on with their murmured conversation as the candle flames flared in the draught from the door.

To hide her initial hesitation Caro crossed the floor with a firm step and took up a position in front of the huge fireplace. Grateful for the warmth she surreptitiously surveyed her companions. Craigraven, with his unusual height dominated the group, while both the other men seemed to be listening intently to his words. Suddenly all three turned to look at her and to her consternation she blushed a fiery red under their concerted gaze.

'This is Mr Dunwoody, our Episcopalian minister,' announced Alan MacKenzie, indicating the stranger. 'You will doubtless be relieved to know that the Episcopalian Church is nearest in form to the Church of England.'

Caro curtsied briefly to the man in black, who bowed in return, the white bands of his collar falling over the leather book clasped to his chest. Dispassionately she thought that he looked as nervous as she felt and wondered briefly what the effect would be if she made her coercion known and asked for his aid, however, one glance at Craigraven's grim expression made her put aside all such thoughts.

In a moment she and the tall Scot were standing side by side, the priest facing them and the others watching from their various positions about the room. Mr Dunwoody began to intone the ceremony in a high-pitched mumble that was almost unintelligible to the English girl and she was taken by surprise when Alan MacKenzie took her hand and slipped a thick gold signet ring on her finger.

Looking down, Caro recognised it as one he wore on his little finger, the metal was still warm and felt heavy and unfamiliar on her hand. In a moment the ceremony seemed over for the minister closed the prayer-book he held and stepped back.

'A dram, Alan—to toast your bride?' asked Christian, her voice wavering slightly. 'It's the custom,' she reminded him, when instead of replying he turned to survey the woman beside him.

'Then we must conform,' he said quietly, his grey eyes glinting frostily down at her. 'Gentlemen,' he said, without removing his gaze, 'A Highland toast, if you please.'

Morag quickly snatched away the glasses already on the table and taking others from a cupboard set them ready. When they were filled each man took one and stepping on to a chair, stood with one foot on the table, amid the debris of the unfinished meal and raised their filled glasses on high.

Craigraven shouted something in Gaelic, loudly repeated by the others, of which the English girl understood only the name MacKenzie, then they all drained the fiery liquid and with one accord turned to fling the glasses into the fireplace.

Staring at the shattered remains, Caro understood the housekeeper's forethought in removing her good crystal from harm, feeling somewhat shaken herself by the barbaric display. Craigraven jumped lightly from his perch and taking her hand, tucked it into his elbow with a proprietary air that made her heart lurch.

'My lady gives you thanks for your presence,' he said to the minister. 'Johnnie MacKenzie will see you on your way, after Morag, here, has given you refreshment—being a man of the world as well as a man of the cloth, you'll understand that I have other business to attend to.'

And with a general bow he and his new bride left the room.

Instead of crossing to the tiny room she had occupied since her arrival, Caro was led into the door opposite Christian's bed chamber. With as much composure as she could manage, she looked calmly about as she advanced into the masculine room. Heavy oak furniture, chosen more for comfort than elegance, and thick, warm hangings presented a different picture from Christian's domain.

Seeing none of this Caroline glanced blindly around, before putting as much space between herself and Craigraven as possible, she crossed to the window. Turning back into the room, she lifted her head and faced him.

'Not like this, Craigraven,' she said.

He made no pretence of misunderstanding, but leaning against the door jamb, folded his arms and raised one eyebrow quizzically. 'Like what, Mistress MacKenzie?' he asked, lightly.

Caro took a deep, uneven breath. 'You know what I mean. We are married—it might as well be for better than worse. We'll have to live together for the rest of our lives . . . h-how we start will make a difference to our future.'

Craigraven unfolded his arms and crossed towards her, stepping so near that she was forced to tilt up her head to meet his eyes.

'You mean you don't want me to force myself upon you,' he said bluntly.

'A—kind lover would be more pleasant,' Caro replied, as calmly as she could. Unable to meet the penetrating grey gaze any longer she lowered her eyelids and hid behind the lashes.

'I've never had to force a lassie yet and I don't intend to start with my wife,' Alan MacKenzie told her and for the first time since the unheralded arrival of Johnnie, Caro felt a faint easing of tension.

She looked up hopefully, 'You mean— you won't . . . that you'll leave without . . .'

Craigraven laughed softly, 'Now, that,' he said, 'would be asking too much,' and tugged gently at the knot of cherry ribbons that fastened her lace fichu.

The gesture should have alarmed the English girl, but strangely it did not, instead she felt the stirring of an unfamiliar emotion deep within her. Her eyes widened and her breath quickened but she did not back away. Craigraven stared down into her eyes, his own narrowed with interest. Deliberately he allowed the back of his hand lightly to brush the first slight swell of her breasts before turning away.

'Let us finish the glass of wine we had started when Jockie interrupted us,' he suggested and Caro heard glass chink as he busied himself at a small table.

Holding two slender glasses filled with an amber liquid, he turned back to the girl, and proffered one. 'Take it,' he said, seeing her hesitation, and somewhat uncertainly she did so. 'To us,' he said, raising his glass to her and waited until she had responded to his toast before swinging away to seat himself in the only chair.

With a commanding gesture, he indicated a little stool at his feet. 'Sit, Mistress MacKenzie,' he said, with an emphasis on the title.

To her surprise Caro found herself flurried into obeying, sitting upright and with as much dignity as she could manage on the low stool. Craigraven's hand settled on her shoulder and drew her to rest against his knee. Caro took an unwary gulp of wine and immediately choked and had to be patted on the back before she recovered.

'Take care, Caro—it would not enhance my reputation if my bride should die of asphyxia on her wedding night,' commented her companion dryly, her christian name sounding oddly on his lips. His fingers toyed with a strand of hair that had escaped from her pins, slowly sliding down across her cheek and then to smooth the curve of her neck.

The caress sent a pleasant shiver down her spine as she closed her eyes, aware for the first time how very enjoyable a man's touch could be. Sensuous delight warmed her as Craigraven's hand drifted across the base of her throat and over the smooth skin below.

When he cupped her chin and bent over her, she gave him her lips willingly, responding eagerly to his kiss. Surprised by the depth of feeling which overwhelmed her, she returned his ardent kisses, catching her breath with pleasure at each new touch of his hand.

Gathering her closer, Alan MacKenzie drew her up to lie across his knees and she hung in his arms, heavy and languorous. With one finger she outlined the suntanned face above her, touching the straight eyebrows, skimming lightly down the thin nose and across the high, tight cheekbones, but when she smoothed the lips, Craigraven caught her hand and nipped her fingertips in a lover's bite.

Watching her face, he tweaked undone the strings that laced her bodice, pulling free the bunch of cherry ribbons that had attracted his attention earlier. When she made no protest, lying still except for a rapidly beating pulse fluttering wildly in her throat, he bent slowly and put his mouth to the gentle swell of her breast.

Lifting her like a child, he stood up and walked to the four-poster bed. Lying her against the piled pillows, he straightened and looked down at her his face in shadow, his fair hair haloed by the candle light.

'Well, Mistress MacKenzie?' he asked, quietly. 'Well? Shall we to bed?'

CHAPTER
EIGHT

AWAKENING the next morning in unfamiliar surroundings Caroline lay still for a moment staring up at the fringed canopy of the strange bed wondering where she was, before the events of the previous night came flooding into her mind.

A wave of warmth washed over her, from her curled toes to her hot cheeks and she stretched languidly, enjoying the feel of the rough linen against her naked body. Recalling overheard remarks that other women had made, she wondered at their professed indifference to love-making thinking that, personally, she had found the experience totally enjoyable.

Sighing with remembered pleasure, she looked round for her partner. Finding the place beside her empty, her eyes wandered from the rumpled sheets across the room, alighting on a figure by the window. Admiring the broad shoulders and slim waist and hips, Caro watched as Craigraven peered intently down into the courtyard.

Suddenly he snatched up his shirt and began to dress hurriedly. As he tucked the voluminous folds into his tight trews her curiosity could be contained no longer.

'What is it?' she asked. 'What's happening?'

'I heard a shot and now they are bringing someone in,' he told her briefly, smiling at her confusion as she sat up abruptly and then realising that she was naked, hurriedly retired under the bedclothes again. 'Remember you are a married woman, now,' he advised, allowing her to read the expression in his eyes, before leaving the room.

Once alone Caroline lay back and gazed thoughtfully up at the bed canopy for some minutes before throwing back the covers, she scrambled out of bed and washed and dressed quickly.

When she entered the great hall the unexpected dramatic scene revealed caused her to draw back in the doorway, one hand covering her mouth as she watched the group by the fireplace. Craigraven, the factor and Johnnie MacKenzie were all grouped together, looking at an unconscious man on the floor at their feet. A bright red stain was spreading over one shoulder of the grey homespun jacket he wore and a livid purple bruise was already swelling above one eye, but it was the pale face that made the English girl hold her breath as her eyes widened; even without his uniform she had no difficulty in recognising Jamie Preston.

'He's a gey bonny fighter. Didn't he put up a fight, just, even after I'd put a hole in him,' Johnnie was saying in English after an excited burst of Gaelic. With one bare foot he stirred the supine figure with a proprietary air.

'Oh, don't,' Caro cried, hurrying forward as the men turned to look at her with surprised expressions. 'The poor man's hurt,' she said, feeling some explanation was needed. 'He'll die if the bleeding isn't stopped.'

With the words, she knelt down beside the Lieutenant, opening his jacket with trembling fingers to reveal a gaping wound still welling blood in a steady stream. Hastily untying his cravat, she folded it into a pad and pressed it over the blackened bullet hole.

Craigraven knelt beside her and slid a hand under James Preston's back. 'The bullet's still in,' he remarked almost conversationally, watching as Caro's hands grew still. 'Tell me, my wee wife,' he went on softly, 'he wouldn't be a friend of yours, now would he?'

'Whatever makes you think that?' she asked unsteadily. 'You must know that I only mix with Redcoats.' Her hand flicked at the grey material.

He did not answer, but after a few seconds' grave regard gave his attention to the unconscious man. 'Bring hot water and towels,' he commanded over his shoulder to the watching men, 'and you, Caro, will help me remove the bullet—and if he answers a few questions while we're doing it, well that will be very convenient.'

Caro shivered at his bland tone. 'I'm not good at this kind of thing,' she said, wishing to escape.

'You seemed to be managing very well, a wee while ago.'

'Y-es, but that was necessary, *this* is—cold-blooded.'

Craigraven looked at her white face and pleading eyes and his own expression softened. 'Off you go then,' he said, 'but send Morag to me and ask her to bring some vinegar, we'll try to bring him round first.'

The English girl hesitated. 'Why vinegar?'

'The smell will bring him out of his swoon,' she was told curtly as her husband cut away the bloodstained shirt.

'You—you don't mean to *torture* him!'

Alan MacKenzie sent her a brief glance. 'I'm no torturer, my lassie—if he should answer freely while I'm attending to his wound, then that's all to the good.'

Leaving him to his task, Caro went in search of the housekeeper and having given her message returned with her.

'Come to keep an eye on the proceedings?' asked Craigraven looking up.

'My help might be needed,' Caro replied, avoiding his question and took up a position by the window. For a while all was quiet behind her, only faint rustles of material disturbing the silence, then a sighing moan carried across the room, making the hair raise on the nape of her neck.

'There, there laddie, you're no so bad,' murmured Craigraven, surprising her by his gentle tone. 'I'm just after the ball my man put into your shoulder.' There was silence for a while, broken by a gasp of pain and then the Scotsman spoke again. 'What's your name my bold fellow?'

'Jamie—James Preston,' she heard the familiar English voice reply.

'And what were you doing here Jamie?'

'I—I was lost—'

'Where were you going?'

'Beauly . . .'

'Were you now,' Craigraven sounded disbelieving. 'Caro,' he called over his shoulder. 'Come here and meet your fellow Sassenach.'

Reluctantly she obeyed, hoping that Jamie would have enough sense to pretend not to recognise her, but when she stopped behind the kneeling Scot, she was relieved to see that the Lieutenant's eyes were closed.

'Too late,' observed Craigraven, ironically. 'The poor laddie's swooned away again.' Wiping his hands he stood up. 'Take him to the turret room,' he commanded. 'It's a grand place for a guest, until we know whether he's a friend or not.'

'Are you still leaving for Inverness?' asked Caroline when they were alone.

'As soon as I've had my breakfast and seen to one or two things.' Craigraven gestured her to the table and held a chair for her.

'P-perhaps I could intercede for your brother,' she offered as she seated herself.

'A niece is not so close as a daughter,' replied her husband, carving cold meat.

'No—but perhaps my uncle would listen to me.'

He shook his head. 'My thanks, lassie, but if he refused he'd be expecting some move from me—I'll just creep in and surprise him.'

'Be careful,' Caro surprised herself by saying.

Craigraven lifted one eyebrow and smiled across the table. 'I've no intention of leaving you a widow, yet a while,' he told her, with a significant gleam in his eyes.

Flushing under the meaning gaze, Caro hastily poured herself a cup of tea and was relieved when the door opened and Christian appeared.

'I've just had a look at that poor laddie you've mistreated,' she said, seating herself at the table.

'Mistreated! What could be kinder than removing a lead ball from his shoulder?'

'Not shooting him at all, brother. What a way to treat a harmless stranger! And we Highlanders proud of our name for hospitality.'

'If he's harmless, then I'm sorry for his reception,' Craigraven said quietly, making his new wife look up quickly. 'But I've an idea that there's more to our visitor than he'd have us think.'

'What nonsense,' she felt called upon to say. 'He looks perfectly ordinary to me.'

'Ordinary!' exclaimed Christian, hectic spots of red colouring her cheeks when two pairs of surprised eyes were turned in her direction. 'I mean . . . he looks a very nice young man,' she explained, stirring her tea vigorously.

'You mean, my love, that your handsome fellow played upon your heartstrings with his pale face and bonny brown hair.'

'Why don't you set out to rescue Rory?' she asked pointedly, giving her attention to her breakfast. Having eaten a meagre meal quickly, she excused herself and left the room hurriedly.

'You'd best away to act duenna to my besotted sister,' Craigraven told Caro, his eyes amused.

The English girl rose, 'You—you won't leave without seeing me.'

Craigraven lifted his head to study her anxious face. 'I'll come to say goodbye,' he told her. 'I'll be a while yet before I leave.'

With the promise she had to be satisfied as he left the room almost immediately. Thoughtfully she headed towards her former room and finding the door open stood outside watching for a moment before she went in. Christian was sitting on the bed, wiping Lieutenant Preston's forehead with a damp cloth, her attitude speaking of care and concern.

'He's awful hot,' she said, looking up as Caro entered. 'It's feverish the poor man is.'

'Well, Johnnie *did* hit him over the head as

well as shooting him,' the English girl pointed out reasonably.

'Jock's ever the one to do things over well . . . and this time I'm afraid he's killed the poor mannie.'

'Oh, no. I'm sure not. Jamie is very—' she broke off, realising what she had said as the other girl looked up. 'I mean he *looks* very strong,' she finished hastily.

'How did you know his name?' Christian asked, puzzled.

'He told us—when Alan asked him,' Caro explained, thankful she could speak the truth.

'Jamie—' repeated Christian. 'It's a good Scots name for all Alan says he's an Englishman.'

'We're nay sae bad,' observed Caro, with a parody of a Scottish accent, hoping to distract the other from her slip, but Christian's attention was solely on the wounded man, her expression tense and anxious as she stared down at him. Caro watched her thoughtfully, struck by the Scots girl's obvious interest in the man who was a stranger to her.

Before she could speak the Lieutenant murmured and began to toss restlessly. With a violent motion he struggled to sit up, fighting against their restraining hands, until with a groan of pain he subsided, beads of sweat shining on his forehead.

'What'll we do, Caro?' asked Christian, her voice tight with anxiety.

'Morag will be here soon with a cooling drink—and in the mean time we can sponge him with a damp cloth as you were doing.'

Suiting the words to actions, she poured water from a jug into a bowl and soaking a cloth wrung it out and passed it to the other girl. As they both turned to the man on the bed an exclamation was startled from them; a pair of puzzled blue eyes were open and wandering round the room with a wide stare.

'Why, Caro,' Jamie Preston said, recognition in his gaze. 'How pleased I am to have found you.'

His words seemed to fill the room to be followed by a horrid silence so tangible that Caro almost felt the atmosphere settle heavily on her shoulders. Christian's soothing hand was arrested in mid-motion as she stared at the English girl, her mouth adroop. Caro's tongue was paralysed and her mind a total blank, while she could only stand stiff and still with dismay. Hearing a movement in the doorway, she knew instinctively who was there and shivered with apprehension as she turned to confront the silent watcher.

Craigraven's grey eyes were bleak and his

expression grim. 'So,' he said harshly. 'It's as I thought, the fellow's no stranger to you.'

'I—do know him,' Caro admitted.

'He's a Redcoat, no doubt.' Her silence was answer enough and his face hardened. 'I should expect deceit and guile from you, but I had hoped that your new circumstances might have roused loyalty—if nothing else.'

She wanted to cry out that he was mistaken, that she would give anything not to see his new softened expression replaced by the icy bleakness with which he was staring at her. Reading the contempt and scorn in his eyes, she bit back the words on her tongue.

'I suppose this was all arranged?'

The unreasonable accusation roused her, and at last she raised her chin and defended herself. 'How could it be?' she demanded shrilly. 'You kidnapped me, remember—*I* didn't inveigle my way into your house in order to spy on you.'

'Who is he?' Alan MacKenzie asked.

'You heard—he's James Preston and he's a Lieutenant in my uncle's regiment. He was Georgina's friend—but why he should take it upon himself to seek me out, I do not know.'

The look he sent her was hard and unyielding. Brushing past her, he stood by the bed looking down at the feverish occupant for a moment. 'I'll get no sense out of him,' he commented more to himself than the watching women. 'I'll leave him in your care Christian,' he said, his expression softening as he bent to kiss his sister. 'I'll bring good news when I return,' he promised, his hand resting momentarily on her shoulder.

Gazing at his wife, the kindness slid from his face. 'A word with you, mistress,' he said curtly and taking her elbow in a grip that let her feel his strength, he walked her from the room.

'Now Mistress Caroline Candover Mac-Kenzie,' he said grimly, when they had reached their own bed chamber. 'I've something to say to you.'

Gathering all her courage Caro lifted her head to meet his gaze and was shaken by the anger and scorn she saw there. Craigraven's grey eyes glittered with cold fury and disillusion, his mouth curved with contempt as he stared down at her.

'You are my wife, may God help me,' he went on in cutting tones, 'to do with as I please. You are my chattel, you belong to me and if I so wish I can make your life so unpleasant that you will wish you had never been born—'

'Alan—believe me, I had no idea that Jamie Preston was following Johnnie—'

'You could have told me who he was—'

'And let you think he was a spy and perhaps ill-treat him!'

'Since when have I treated a wounded man badly?'

'You were none too kind to the Lieutenant,' Caro pointed out quickly.

'That's as may be—what is in question is your loyalty to me.'

'How can I be loyal to you, when I hardly know you?' she asked, exasperated.

'I was foolish enough to think that you cared for me, that a fondness had grown between us despite our differences.'

'Oh, *Alan!*' She would have gone to him, but his cold expression and immobile stance repelled her and her movement was still-born, scarcely stirring her skirts before she was still again.

'But I see that I was mistaken,' he went on inexorably, 'and that you are as treacherous as all your perfidious race.'

'I haven't noticed much loyalty among the Scots,' she was stung into retorting. 'You talk a lot about your clans and chiefs, but when it comes to actually showing your colours, all your so-called loyalty vanishes and you stay at home to keep your estates safe or fight among yourselves like a lot of savages.'

Craigraven glared at her, his nostrils flaring with disdain. 'Think of my return, madam,' he advised bitingly, 'for return I shall and when I do I shall take steps to make you a dutiful wife!'

With the words, he swung on his heel and strode from the room, his shoulder plaid flaring out like a tartan banner. Caro's knees gave way abruptly and she sank heavily on to the bed, weak from the furious encounter; never before had she either felt or been the recipient of such rage and the violent emotion left her sick and shaken.

By evening she had made up her mind; however difficult her task, she would not wait calmly for Alan MacKenzie. Come what may he would not find her at Craigraven Tower on his return and with this in mind she set about devising some means of escape. The fact that she could not leave James Preston behind made the endeavour harder to accomplish and at first she despaired of finding a means of removing the wounded man from the stronghold, but just when she was on the point of abandoning the project for the time being, the way was suddenly cleared.

Not only had Jamie Preston's fever abated on the day Craigraven set out on his journey, within a few days the soldier's strength returning, but to her amazement Caro saw that Christian was deeply attracted by the young man. Watching silently she saw the Scots girl blossom under the smiling gaze of the Lieutenant and was surprised and touched by their obvious growing regard for each other.

'What would Craigraven say?' she asked at last, feeling the question would make Christian realise that her affection was clear for all to see and also that the other's answer might help solve her own problem.

Alan MacKenzie's sister smiled gently, her mouth soft with secret dreams. 'Quite a lot no doubt,' she said, 'but for once in my life I've no mind to heed my big brother. As soon as he returns we shall tell Alan of our love and hope he will be kind to us—if not, then we shall leave here and I will follow the drum with my husband.'

Her pale eyes sparkled with resolution and on impulse Caro put her arms round the Scots girl and hugged her tightly. 'What a brave girl,' she commented, kissing her. 'I'm so pleased for you—I hope you will be very happy.'

Privately she was a little disquieted at the apparent ease with which the soldier fell in and out of love, and as soon as she could, tackled him upon the matter of her cousin.

'I'll not deny that I found Miss Georgie attractive and would willingly have made her my wife if it had been possible,' Lieutenant Preston told her honestly, 'but we both knew that marriage was out of the question. It was something we had to accept and that coloured our relationship. The feeling I have for Christian is much deeper. We are in love and intend to wed no matter what.'

He spoke with quiet conviction and Caro had no difficulty in believing his sincerity. 'Alan KacKenzie will not be pleased,' she said simply.

'Of course we hope the matter can be accomplished without upsetting the family, but if not, then we arrange things ourselves—whatever happens she will not be forced to marry a man she has no liking for.'

'Campbell Frazer is well thought of by Craigraven—by my husband.'

'Perhaps—but from what Christian tells me I think he is not as loyal to Craigraven as he would have us believe,' was the unequivocal reply.

Caro reflected that the Scots girl seemed to have taken Lieutenant Preston into her confidence as quickly as into her heart and, wondering a little at such unexpected behaviour, went in search of a quiet spot where she could order her thoughts without interruption.

The walled garden seemed the ideal place and she hurried down the winding turn-pike stairs and out of the tower before any should stop her. Once in the garden and out of sight of the house, she sought Christian's favourite seat and perching herself on the hard stone she scuffed her heels in the shingle path and watched the black toes of her shoes swing backwards and forwards under the hem of her blue skirt.

So much had happened so quickly that her mind and emotions were in turmoil; a short while before she had, to her own amazement, been ready to love her husband believing that he loved her in return. Now she hardly knew her own feelings, save that rather than face Alan MacKenzie's obvious dislike and scorn, she would sooner leave Craigraven Tower for ever—even if it meant that her bones, picked clean by the buzzards, would be found some day on the mountainside.

She was unaware of the single tear that had fallen from her long lashes, until it had trickled down her cheek to tickle the corner of her mouth. Licking it away with the tip of her tongue she sniffed dolefully, thinking of what might have been. For a moment she could almost hear the happy sound of children playing about her feet and when she heard the sound of footsteps on the path, she looked up with a dreamy smile, half expecting Craigraven to join his imagined family. Instead the sight of Campbell Frazer regarding her steadily brought her back abruptly to reality.

'Craigraven said you were not to leave the tower,' he said, his tone expressionless.

'And—do you always do what Craigraven says?' she asked quietly.

The factor's gaze sharpened, interest flickering at the back of his veiled eyes.

'It's yourself we are talking of,' he replied.

Caro shook her head, 'No, Mr Frazer it is *you*.'

'Then you will have to be clearer,' he said, after a while, during which he had studied her thoughtfully.

Taking a deep breath Caro plunged on, encouraged by his attitude. 'I believe, Mr Frazer, that you are not over enamoured of my husband,' she said recklessly.

Campbell Frazer's eyes narrowed and his mouth curved in what might have been a thin smile. Relaxing, he folded his arms and leaned back against one of the arms of the stone seat.

'What a strange assumption,' he remarked

easily. 'Whatever gives you that idea, Mistress MacKenzie?'

'Several things—tales I've heard, remarks made—your expression at times. You do not always regard your chief with kind eyes, Frazer the factor.'

The look he turned on her was far from kind, sending an icy finger of anticipation between her shoulder blades, but she kept her eyes on his, meeting his gaze steadily.

'I prefer to be known by my name,' he said thinly, showing his teeth in a tight smile.

'Precisely,' Caro commented, meaningly. 'Cease play-acting *Mr* Frazer—I think we understand each other well enough.'

He shrugged. 'Perhaps—but be a little more precise, mistress, if you please.'

'I wish to leave here, Mr Frazer and I've an idea you would be willing to help me.'

Campbell Frazer surveyed the garden with interest. 'And what do I get in return?' he asked casually, turning his attention to his finger nails.

'Why—the pleasure of having bested Craigraven. Think how . . . *upset* he will be when he discovers I have gone. And,' she went on delicately, 'if *that* is not enough for you, I dare say my uncle can be persuaded to further the career of one who was the means of restoring his niece to him.'

Making her a gallant bow, the factor carried her hand to his lips. 'I never could refuse a lassie my aid,' he said, with sentiment.

Twitching her fingers out of his grasp Caro stood up. 'We will leave as soon as possible—Craigraven will not be over-long about his errand,' she said briskly, scarcely bothering to hide the sudden dislike she felt of the man beside her.

'Tonight then—tomorrow will be too late—'

'We must take the Lieutenant with us. I will not leave him here to be the object of Craigraven's wrath.'

'A wounded man will hold us up—what if we meet MacKenzie on the road?'

'Jamie Preston comes with us,' Caro told him decisively.

'Then we'll have to take the mountain pass.'

The English girl smiled. 'It sounds delightful, Mr Frazer,' she said.

CHAPTER
NINE

'It's best that we leave at night then—the servants and men are loyal to Craigraven. The longer we have before they discover we are gone, the longer it will take for them to alert the MacKenzie.' The factor looked at her with unfriendly eyes. 'Make your preparations with discretion and be ready to leave at midnight.'

With a curt bow, he swung round and hurried away, leaving Caro in no doubt that in allowing her dislike to show, she had made an enemy. Jumping to her feet, she lifted her skirts high and ran in search of Christian. She found the Scots girl in her room, with the Lieutenant ensconced in the armchair. They were holding hands and seemed engrossed in each other's company, looking up with preoccupied expressions at her entry.

'What a pair of lovebirds,' she could not forbear from saying and was at once contrite as two identical waves of colour spread over the faces turned to her. 'Forgive me, but you *do* look rather involved. I wouldn't interrupt but for the fact that . . . for my own reasons I must leave the tower and I can't leave Jamie here to bear the brunt of Alan's anger.'

Christian's eyes widened. 'Whatever do you mean? *Leave* here when you're the mistress of Craigraven. You're wed with my brother, Caro, you cannot leave!'

'I must,' the English girl told her doggedly. 'Alan has made it plain that he only married me to make sure I could not give evidence against him, should matters ever come to court.'

For a moment her unhappy despair showed. 'Oh, Christian,' she cried, 'I cannot—*will* not have a marriage of convenience. If you love your Jamie, you must know that.'

The other girl searched her face and reading the blind misery there, hurried across the room to put her arms comfortingly round her.

'I do understand, my poor lassie,' she whispered, 'but will this no blow over? Alan ever had a fine temper, but it was gone as quickly as it was raised.'

Caro shook her head wretchedly. 'No,' she murmured sadly. 'This is no trivial matter. We both said unforgivable things. Our marriage was a terrible mistake. I thought we l-loved each other, but our backgrounds, loyalties—everything we believe—are too different to make it possible.'

Christian smoothed her hair. 'I think you are mistaken, but if you feel like that maybe it's better that you *do* leave—if only for a while.'

'I can't leave Jamie here,' cried Caro, looking up.

'No more can you,' Christian agreed at once. 'Now what's to do? I'll come with you, but we'll need help.'

'Campbell Frazer is arranging things.'

The other girl frowned. 'Is that wise?'

Caro spread her hands. 'Who else?' she asked.

'I wish you would not talk as if I were not here,' complained Lieutenant Preston. 'Have I no say in the matter?'

'Jamie, my dear, as brave and bold a fellow as yourself is no much use when he's weak from a recent wound. We need an able-bodied man to guide us over the mountains and even I am not sure of the path.' She turned to Caro. 'I presume that is the way Campbell intends to go?'

Caro nodded. 'He said we could be sure of avoiding Craigraven that way.'

The Scots girl considered, 'Well, there's no saying he won't come that way if he takes a mind to it, but I suppose it would be easier to hide from him on the hills, provided we saw him coming.'

'We'll leave after midnight the factor said.'

'He's awful willing,' commented the other uneasily. 'It's a gey pity we need him. I do not trust that wee mannie.'

Caroline was inclined to agree with her, but said nothing, instead, advising them both to make their preparations with caution, went to her own room to make ready herself.

With a shock she realised that she had brought nothing of her own to Craigraven Keep; her possessions had all been given to her by the inmates of the tower, a bone comb from Christian, soap and towels from Morag, a silver brooch from Alan. With a gentle finger she touched the ornate silver shield encircling the brownish-yellow stone then, almost defiantly, she pinned it on to her bodice and using a square scarf, tied her other possessions into a secure bundle.

Careful to keep their intentions secret they went about their preparations without even the housekeeper being aware of their activities. By nightfall all was in readiness and an unfamiliar quietness fell over the tower as if even the ancient stone keep was waiting in anticipation.

Unwilling for company, Caro shut herself in the room she had so lately shared with Alan MacKenzie and did her best to keep her thoughts from the brief happiness she had found there. Against her will her mind returned again and again to the moments of shared bliss when their love had seemed mutual and lasting. Even now she found it almost impossible to accept that it had been so transient, so fragile, but after the violent quarrel that had taken place between them, she knew that the love Craigraven had professed to feel for her and the words of affection he had breathed in her ear had been nothing more than pretence to gain his own safety.

Cursing herself for a willing dupe, she flung a book at her reflection in the mirror on the wall and as the glass shattered into a thousand shining slivers threw herself face down on the bed and gave herself up to an orgy of tears, crying with a wild abandon she had not felt since her childhood.

Slowly the hours crept towards midnight and when, at last, the long-case clock in the great hall struck twelve, she sighed with relief that the waiting was over. Swinging her legs over the side of the bed, she fastened the plaid shawl about her shoulders, gathered up her few belongings and quietly left the room without a backward glance.

Christian and Jamie Preston were already in the darkened hall and as she arrived, Campbell Frazer entered by the other door.

'All's ready,' he announced quietly and a tingle of anticipation found its way down the English girl's back.

'So are we,' she replied, a hint of defiance in her voice making her speak more loudly than she intended.

'Ssh—ssh,' came Christian's sibilant whisper.

'Then we'll away before you wake the others,' said the factor, taking the English girl's arm and leading the way down the spiral stairs, sure-footed in the darkness.

The others followed him more cautiously, holding their breath and straining their ears for sounds of discovery. To Caro's surprise the iron yett was not in place and the stout wooden door opened easily to Campbell Frazer's touch.

'I opened it on my rounds,' he observed, evidently sensing her surprise. He laughed quietly, a sound that made her shiver. 'It's part of my duty to make sure the tower is secure for the night!'

'Then lock it behind us,' she told him sharply.

'Och, aye and isn't it my intention? If they're locked in, it will take them longer to set out in pursuit.'

'You are very astute, Mr Frazer.'

'It pays—in my line of business.'

Disliking his proximity and the familiarity with which he had taken her arm, Caro freed herself under the pretence of turning back to aid Christian and Jamie.

'I begin to understand your feelings for Campbell Frazer,' she told Christian under her breath.

'Do you, indeed?' Craigraven's sister was interested. 'I thought I was the only person not to be charmed by him.'

'At first I rather liked him, but somehow lately, I've changed my views.'

'In that case I've something to tell you later,' was Christian's enigmatic reply as the factor motioned for them to wait in the shadows of the castle walls, while he cautiously crossed the courtyard and vanished like a wraith into the stables.

So quickly, that the horses must have been bridled and waiting, he returned leading four of the sturdy little garrons, their unshod hoofs scarcely making more than a clicking sound on the cobbles.

'Mount up,' he commanded in an impatient whisper and leaving the Englishman to climb into the rough saddle as best he could, Campbell Frazer pushed Caro on to the broad back of her pony and then performed the same service for Christian. Without more ado, he kicked his own mount into motion and led the little cavalcade at a quick trot away from the tower.

Not until they had taken the rough track along which she had ridden on her previous outing with the factor and the keep lay white and sleeping below them, did Caro feel free to relax somewhat. Glancing down she saw the stout walls gleaming palely in the moonlight and felt a hastily denied twinge of sorrow at leaving the ancient building and all it had once seemed to offer.

A muffled call attracted her attention and, looking up, she saw that the factor was gesturing her to join the others who had ridden on. Kicking her heels into the broad sides of her pony she urged him into an uncomfortable trot and soon was riding behind Christian, who had been bringing up the rear.

'Are you sad to be leaving the tower?' she asked over her shoulder. 'Or are you sorry you've quarrelled with my brother?'

Caro looked at her, feeling the anger that had cooled a little rising again. 'You must know that your brother is the most odious, ruthless, arrogant man,' she said coldly. 'If I hurt your feelings, then I apologise, but he cheated me into believing that he—h-had an affection for me, when in reality he wanted us to wed so that I could not give evidence against him and so that he could keep me a prisoner if he wished.' She looked away, her eyes blinded by tears, but whether of rage or sadness she could not tell.

'I think he would not have married without some feeling for you—'

'Tush!' The word exploded across the other's quick tones, startling in the silence. Caro angrily brushed aside the glittering drops and lifted her chin. 'Craigraven feels nothing—his heart is like a cruel black stone!' And jabbing with her heels she goaded her garron to greater effort and passing Christian and the Englishman, joined Campbell Frazer at the head of the little band.

'Cannot we make better speed?' she asked, impatiently.

He glanced significantly over his shoulder. '*You* brought the others,' he pointed out. 'The man is feeling his wound already and it's a good while since Christian has sat a horse—or had you forgotten?'

Biting her lip, Caro was silent; she *had*

forgotten and now blamed herself for her
thoughtlessness. Without considering the
difficulties for anyone else, she had forced
them to concede to her desires. Blinded by
her own rage and despair she had thought of
nothing save the fact that she could not face
Alan MacKenzie's perfidy.

With a smothered exclamation she dragged round the pony's head and waited for the
Scots girl to come up. Looking at her with
new eyes she could see that the other rode
with obvious discomfort.

'Oh, Christian!' she cried, contritely, seizing the other's bridle. 'How could I have
been so thoughtless! I quite forgot about
you—not riding, about your leg and here I
am dragging you along these wild tracks with
no consideration.'

Christian gave her a tired smile. 'I would
not have come if I had not wanted to,' she
said simply. 'If you went, then Jamie could
not be left to face Alan's wrath.'

'I should have stayed,' Caro cried, wretchedly.

The other shook her head, 'No—Craigraven has had too much of his own head. It's
time he learnt that others' opinions and
wishes are as important as his. With luck the
surprise of this will make him think and
perhaps he'll be a nicer person.'

'You can manage? Your leg's not paining you?'

'Alan said it was all nerves and I only had to try. And,' Christian confided thoughtfully, 'and do you know, I've an inkling he may have been right? I'm tired and my leg is stiff, but to be honest, it's none so bad. It's even a wee bittie pleasant to be back on a horse.'

'You're sure?'

'Och, aye, but I'm no so sure of Jamie.'

Following her gaze, Caro could understand her anxiety; the soldier was riding slouched in the saddle, his head hanging and his fingers entwined in his mount's shaggy mane.

'We must stop!' she cried, plunging ahead to speak to the factor.

'Indeed we must not,' was his calm reply, without slowing the speed of his mount.

'But Jamie Preston—the Lieutenant is near swooning,' she protested.

Sparing the briefest glance over his shoulder the man shrugged indifferently. 'Didn't I tell you he'd slow us? We are still within reach of the castle. If it's discovered that we are gone they could still catch us.' His pale eyes held hers significantly. 'If you've a wish to be taken back to face Craigraven on his return, I do not share it.'

'I—would prefer not,' she faltered.

'Then we must continue,' he told her and taking her compliance for granted, kicked the animal he rode into a more speedy trot.

'He says we are too near the keep to rest yet,' Caro told Christian as the others rode up.

The Lieutenant raised his head and gave them a strained smile. 'Don't worry,' he told them. 'I can manage. We military men can sleep in the saddle, you know.'

'A very useful attribute,' agreed Caro, responding to his effort to ease their worry. 'I *did* purloin Craigraven's pocket flask,' she went on, producing it triumphantly.

'But more important, my dear Caroline, did you think to fill it?' asked the Redcoat, eyeing the silver bottle hopefully.

'Indeed, I did—with his best whisky.'

The soldier accepted it gratefully, choking slightly over the fiery liquid and wishing audibly that it had been brandy.

'What could be better than the water of life?' asked Christian with mock indignation.

They all laughed and after that Caro noticed that although the two women rode either side of the wounded officer in case of need, he seemed cheered by their presence and despite his weakness managed to keep his seat until the factor called a halt in the early hours of the morning. The short Highland night was already ending and pale fingers of pink were beginning to stretch across the sky as they spread their plaids on the damp ground and lay down for a few hours' sleep.

Looking up at the luminous sky, hanging over them like a canopy of shot silk, Caro was inevitably reminded of those other nights she had spent under the stars and against her wish her thoughts turned to Craigraven. Pain that was almost physical in its intensity shot through her making her wince and bite her lip before she deliberately filled her mind with other matters.

Christian and James Preston seemed to fall asleep easily, lying close together, peaceful tartan bundles, but for the English girl oblivion was hard to woo and she found herself again and again staring up at the sky with dry eyes, her mind a hive of muddled, unhappy thoughts. At last she flung aside the blanket and wrapping it around her shoulders went to sit on a nearby boulder.

Only behind her did the ground rise any higher and from her eyrie she could see the surrounding undulating hills and glens, with the occasional silver gleam of a loch or smaller lochan.

Gradually the beauty of the peaceful scene soothed her and for the first time she admitted to herself that she had found an unexpected strength and happiness in the wild Highlands; a sense of security and belonging that she had never felt elsewhere. The austere countryside that at first had appeared harsh and cruel, now seemed merely satisfyingly natural and untamed. As if to emphasise the point a large brown bird, with a cruel curved beak and yellow hooked talons seemed to rise up below her and hang effortlessly as it hovered above its prey.

'An eagle,' observed a voice beside her and turning her head she saw that the factor had joined her while her attention had been on the bird and its environment.

They watched silently as it swooped down, struck, and rose up again, a rabbit hanging from its claws. Caro shivered at such ruthless efficiency, reminded of Craigraven and at last understanding the significance of the eagle's feather pinned in the Highland Chieftain's bonnet.

'He's a braw fellow, there's no doubt,' said Campbell Frazer, grim satisfaction in his tones.

'Who?' she asked involuntarily, her thoughts still with Craigraven and surprised by the factor's description of a man he was betraying.

'Yon eagle, lassie—who else?' His sidelong glance was amused as if he had an inkling of where her thoughts had been.

'It's a pity you kill such a magnificent creature just to use his feathers for adornment.'

'Is that what you were after thinking—and there was I believing it was the MacKenzie you had in mind as you watched the big birdie!'

Ignoring his jibe she gathered her plaid closer about her shoulders and turned to walk back to the campsite, but the factor put out a detaining hand.

'One moment, mistress!' he said, releasing her as she looked pointedly at his fingers on her arm. 'I must ride out to make sure the way is free ahead. With a wounded man and two women we could not ride quickly nor hide easily if the need arose, therefore, it is better to make certain that—*no one*,' he emphasised the word, 'is on our path.'

'You think Craigraven could be ahead?'

'Maybe—maybe not, but it's best to be safe and avoid him if possible. I, for one, would not care to meet him in the circumstances.'

'It would certainly be difficult to find an excuse for our presence,' she agreed.

He nodded. 'So—I'll away and leave you to wake the others when the day breaks and be ready to set out with all speed when I return. It would only be sensible, mind, to keep out of sight, you understand. And if you *should* see the man himself then take my advice, lassie, and take care he doesna' see you.'

He gave emphasis to each word and Caro nodded her agreement, remembering Craigraven's fierce temper and well aware of how it would flare if he should discover their defection.

'You would not find me such a difficult man,' the factor said quietly.

Caro looked up quickly, startled to find him so close as she had momentarily forgotten his presence. 'What do you mean?'

He smiled wryly at her bewilderment. 'I mean, mistress, that you will have need of a protector, having discarded your husband, and that I am ready to offer myself for such a position. I daresay your uncle would be willing to provide for a man who takes you off his hands.'

'Then you mistake General Candover,' said the English girl, soundly. 'And do I have no say in the matter?'

'You've had one chance, lassie and I'd say were no over wise in your choice. You'd do fine with me.'

Caro faced him squarely. 'I'd say you were keener on angering Craigraven, than you are on caring for me!'

Campbell Frazer chuckled. 'You may be right, but I'm no saying,' he told her and obviously well pleased with himself made a mocking bow before mounting his little pony, he trotted off and was soon lost to sight amid the folds and crannies of the rough mountain pass.

Caroline waited a while, pondering on the odd events of the last few weeks until the sun had risen and then woke the others.

'I wonder where the fellow's gone?' murmured the Redcoat as he munched the oat-cakes and curd cheese provided for breakfast.

'He said he was going to make sure the way ahead was safe,' Caro told him.

Christian gave a disparaging smile and licked the crumbs from her fingers.

'Don't you trust him?' the English girl asked.

Christian returned her gaze steadily, before deliberately shaking her head.

'You'd best tell her, my love,' interposed the soldier quietly, the fact that he so obviously knew more than she, making Caro realise how quickly the relatively new relationship between the other girl and the Englishman had developed.

She turned enquiring eyes on Christian and waited for her explanation. The Scots girl busied herself gathering together the breakfast things, giving herself time to assemble her thoughts.

'When Campbell first came to the tower as a boy . . . I did not take to him,' she said at last. 'I tried to like him—to be sorry for the unfortunate circumstances that had brought him—but he always seemed too eager to please, too quick to make himself useful—indispensable. And yet, with all his apparent helpfulness and willing personality somehow after he came, we were always quarrelling among ourselves. My father and Alan were suddenly watchful and wary, as if they no longer trusted each other. Rory and Alan fought and to me it seemed Campbell was the cause behind this mischief. I thought he was the instigator.' She looked up, her eyes shadowed. 'Perhaps I was wrong and it was only that we were all growing up, but one thing I am not wrong about. I *know* that he was the cause of my accident.'

'Christian!' Caro was shocked into exclaiming. 'But you said you were riding

Alan's horse. The factor cannot have meant you to fall if he did not know you were to ride it.'

The other girl met her eyes significantly, her lips tight.

Caro drew in her breath with sudden understanding. 'You mean—Alan! *Alan* was the proposed victim!'

'With Rory betrayed and a prisoner about to be executed, if Alan was . . . out of the way, then only I was left to inherit the castle and lands of Craigraven—and I could, doubtless, be persuaded to marry the factor.'

'It can't be true—it's like a melodrama. Such things don't happen—'

Christian drew herself up and for the first time Caro was aware that she, too, possessed the touchy, Highland pride.

'Oh, I don't mean I don't believe you,' she cried, touching her arm, 'just—that it seems impossible.'

'People have done more for wealth,' put in James Preston. 'Money has been the cause of many a dishonourable deed.'

'What shall we do—what is he doing at this moment?' wondered Caroline, jumping to her feet and pacing impatiently about. 'I have the horridest feeling that he is about some mischief. When he left his manner disturbed me—he seemed anxious and yet eager and excited at the same time.'

Always impulsive, she bit her finger with impatience, while working out some action to take. 'You two hide out of sight and I'll follow him and see what he is doing.'

'I cannot allow you to go tramping about the countryside unattended,' protested the soldier, struggling to his feet, doing his best to hide his pain and weariness from the previous ride.

'Be sensible, Jamie,' said Caro gently. 'You are not fit to ride. Admit it. Stay here with Christian and I promise not to go far and to be back soon. Christian, tell him it's the only thing to do.'

Christian hesitated and then nodded her agreement. 'But keep to the track. Give me your word not to wander. Can you whistle?'

Caro was startled by the question and then grinned and placing two fingers in her mouth gave vent to a shrill sound; a skill learned in her childhood.

Christian nodded. 'Good. When we were children Alan, Rory and I had a signal, like this,' she demonstrated a sharp sound that rose and fell. 'If you have the need use it and I—or someone—will hear it.'

Caroline knew that by 'someone' she

meant Craigraven, a fact which made her pause.

'Promise,' insisted Alan MacKenzie's sister, 'or we both will go with you, something you know fine Jamie is not fit for—or we *all* will stay here.'

Frowning, Caro tried to stare down the other, but Christian held her gaze, refusing to submit and at last the English girl was forced to agree reluctantly. 'Oh, very well, though you must know that I do not care to be coerced,' she said shortly, and walking quickly across to the garrons jerked impatiently at the tether that held her mount.

'Do not be angry, Caro,' implored Christian, touching her arm. 'It's worried I am, about you.'

At once Caro was contrite for her show of ill temper and hugged the other girl impulsively. 'What a wretch I am,' she chided herself. 'It was—'

'I know, I should not have mentioned my brother, though if his name arouses such anger in you, I believe you are not so cold towards him as you would have us believe.'

Choosing to ignore her friend's teasing Caroline climbed on to her pony's broad back and gathered up the crude bridle. 'I'll be back as soon as possible,' she promised. 'If Mr Frazer should return first, then make some excuse for my going ahead.' She smiled wickedly down at the Scots girl, her eyes alight with amusement. '*That*, my dear Christian, shall be *your* part of the endeavour.'

With a wave of her hand, she kicked her heels into the round sides of her mount, who broke into jerky motion and carried her along the track, round an outcrop of broken rock and out of sight.

CHAPTER
TEN

ROUNDING the jagged boulders that had
blocked the view, Caro was amazed to find
an open panorama spread out before her as
the twisting valley with its undulating hill-
ocks fell away at her feet while the encircling
hills rose clear and detailed towards the blue
arched sky. Every colour stood out bril-
liantly as if wet from some artist's paint-
brush, each dusty, pebble-strewn track was
clearly etched, each leaf and flower newly
bright.

Shading her eyes against the brilliance,
she searched for the horse and man she knew
must be somewhere ahead and at last found
Campbell Frazer sitting motionless in the
shadow of a craggy pinnacle overlooking the
rough road. Intrigued by the stillness with
which he waited, Caro watched intently,
realising after a while that he was waiting for
someone. Eager to keep out of sight and yet
determined to see whoever it was the factor
was meeting, she studied the terrain careful-

ly, seeing with pleasure that she could make her way above the watcher.

Tethering her pony to a stunted tree, rooted precariously in a rocky fissure, she left her hiding place and creeping from boulder to boulder carefully drew nearer the factor. Once above him she found that, not only could she recognise the tension with which he awaited his visitor, but also that most of the winding road he watched was clearly visible. After a while, during which she grew impatient, wondering if she was wasting her time, she was alerted by the sound of horses approaching, their hoofs muffled by the dusty path. Campbell Frazer rose to his feet, peering from his hiding place, and when a troop of Redcoats rode into sight he stepped forward, leaving Caro in no doubt that his awaited visitors had arrived.

One hand pressed to her open mouth Caro watched astounded as she crouched in her hiding place. Too far away to hear their words, she saw the officer and Campbell Frazer confer together while the mounted soldiers waited with indifferent patience, then at a word from their leader, they dispersed among the rocks and boulders, leaving the scene as empty of human life as it had been before their arrival.

Whistling to himself as if well pleased, the factor untied his garron and mounting, rode off in the direction from which the soldiers had come, leaving the English girl in no doubt about his intentions. For a moment Caro was indecisive, debating her action before she ran back to her pony, scrambled on to his back and, careful to keep out of sight of the hidden soldiers, urged him round the other side of the intervening outcrop of rock, cut across the countryside and joined up with the track again, hoping she was ahead of the treacherous factor.

Wondering at her own actions, she pushed the little horse to the limit of its capabilities, jogging along at an uncomfortable speed, as its neat, tiny hoofs kicked up spurts of dust with each step. Suddenly her eyes widened in dismay; far ahead and on quite another track a figure could be seen speeding along. Even at that distance, his flying fair hair and familiar figure were clearly recognisable and Caro realised despairingly that in her haste to find Craigraven she had taken the wrong path and that her husband was hurrying to his capture or death. She had hoped that at least he would be accompanied by his loyal retainer, but there was no sign of Johnnie MacKenzie.

Pulling the garron to a halt she slid from

his back and watched the man below. Glancing anxiously back over her shoulder, she thought she could hear someone coming and in desperation put both fingers in her mouth and whistled as Christian had taught her that morning.

Almost as soon as the shrill signal had left her lips, the man below looked up searching the hills above him. Pulling the fichu from her neck, Caro waved it above her head and was rewarded by an answering lift of the hand. Craigraven spun his horse and leaving the road plunged towards her, his mount picking its way among the tumbled rock and tufted grass.

'Well done, lassie—now I'll just wait for himself to fall into my hands,' said a voice behind her and turning Caro was surprised to find Campbell Frazer perched on a nearby boulder hidden from Craigraven's sight.

'I wouldn't do that if I were you,' he advised quietly as she spun round again taking a breath to shout a warning.

He raised his hand and she saw that he held a heavy black pistol, its long barrel menacing her. His eyes in his taut blank face were so cold and his hand so steady that she knew he would kill her without compunction.

'A-Alan would hear the shot,' she pointed out, her voice shaking.

A grim smile crossed the factor's face. 'He'd still come,' he said and she knew he was right. 'Did you think I had no seen you? These eyes of mine can see a buzzard when it's no bigger than the eye of a needle.'

'How nice for you,' Caro remarked politely. 'With such talents you are wasted as a mere factor on a Highland estate!'

Missing the sarcasm in her tone, Campbell Frazer agreed with a nod.

'It's Laird, I should be—and that's precisely my aim.' His eyes left the approaching figure for a moment to slide consideringly over her. 'And with you as wife, I'll double my right to the lands of Craigraven.'

Hoping to keep his attention Caro drew herself to her full height, staring haughtily down her nose at the Scots man. 'And do you suppose for one moment that I'd even *dream* of marrying you, you treacherous little man?'

For a moment she thought she had succeeded in distracting him from his purpose but he only gestured her to his side with the pistol. 'You'll have no choice my bonnie lass,' he told her with grim purpose, most of his attention centred once again on the climbing horse and rider.

'Come closer, my dear one,' whispered her companion, enforcing his command with a jerk of his weapon and reluctantly Caro obeyed, losing sight of her husband as she did so.

The muffled, uneven drum of the garron's hoofs carried clearly to the listeners and then suddenly the horse and rider were in the clearing. For one second Caro met Craigraven's eyes reading first surprise and then dawning comprehension and distaste as he looked from her to the pistol in the factor's hand.

'No—no,' she cried, stepping forward, 'it's not like that—I didn't betray you—'

'Don't believe her, Alan MacKenzie,' said Campbell Frazer easily. 'She couldn't wait for you to leave in case our plan misfired.'

Grey eyes swept Caro contemptuously before turning his shoulder he gave the factor his attention. 'What do you want Factor?' he asked coldly, sliding down from the wide back of his pony.

'Why—your head, I suppose, if that's what is necessary to ensure the reward for a rebel.'

'So,' Craigraven said heavily, looking down at the man in the open ground, 'I should have believed my sister when she said you were rightly named—*Campbell*!'

'Christian never liked me—it would have been much easier if she had. If she'd married me, I'd have had some position and not just been dependent upon your goodwill.'

He spat out the word as if it left a vile taste in his mouth and Craigraven viewed him with interest.

'I see now that you were ever deceitful and conniving,' he commented almost conversationally. 'It was my death or maiming you intended when Christian fell from my horse—and now I put my mind to it, there are other instances of strange accidents, even when we were children.'

Campbell Frazer laughed bitterly. 'I served my apprenticeship, Craigraven, and now I've won. When your head is on Inverness Bridge *I* shall be Laird of Craigraven with a bonnie English wife and a wealthy influential English uncle.'

'I had no idea you were so ambitious as to wish for my inheritance—or that you were such a treacherous *dhu coo*!' observed Craigraven lapsing into his native Gaelic in his anger.

'Black cur, am I? Well, it's as good a name as any,' shrugged the factor. 'Now *mo ghoal*,' he said to Caro, 'tie his hands behind his back.' Dropping his voice so that she alone could hear he added, 'Do as I say, or

I'll shoot him and ravish you without the benefit of a ceremony.'

Caro shuddered and looked away. 'What shall I use?' she asked tonelessly.

'Anything, dolt. His cravat—your neckerchief.'

Dragging her feet, she went to obey, knowing that Alan would think her one with the factor and yet unable to rectify his supposition.

'*Mo ghoal*, is it? My dear one,' he asked, as she pulled the length of linen from about his neck. 'What right has he to call you so?'

'It's more than you ever did,' she replied, pulling his hands behind his back and twisting the scarf about his wrists.

'I'd have called you *bronag beag*, my little darling, or even *ghoal mo chridhe*, which means love of my heart had we time,' his voice was deep and caressing and sent a shiver of unexpected delight down her backbone. 'But that was before I knew you had a liking for this deceitful hound.'

Flinching from the sudden harshness of his voice, she knotted the ends of the cravat and looked across at the factor.

'And his feet,' he said. 'Sit down, Craigraven.'

With difficulty Alan MacKenzie obeyed

him and Caro used his wide leather belt to bind his ankles together.

'Now, I'll just take a wee look to make sure you've done your work well,' said the factor, as she had suspected he would.

With the words Caro drew back her hand and struck Craigraven across the mouth with all her strength. 'No need,' she cried. 'Do you think I'd let a man who treated me like a kitchen wench escape? He's trussed like a chicken, take my word for it,' and scrambling to her feet, she kicked her supine husband in the ribs with the toe of her stout brogue, making him grunt with pain.

'Well, well,' sneered Campbell Frazer. 'I see you have not won the heart of your lady.'

Without waiting for his command, Caroline went to her pony and climbed on to his back. With a glance at Craigraven, who lay watching her, the imprint of her hand like a red scar across his face, she kicked her heels against the garron's hairy stomach and trotted down the hill to join the road along which Craigraven had been travelling.

'You surprise me,' remarked Campbell, joining her in a flurry of small stones and dust.

She did not spare him a glance. 'Don't think I've joined you,' she told him bluntly. 'Craigraven means nothing to me, but you mean even less. For the moment I've sided with you, but you'll have to make it worth my while before I'll marry you.'

The factor looked surprised, startled by her matter of fact attitude. 'I want the Lairdship,' he said after a while, 'and you'll need a husband and position. I don't think you'd care for the life of a poor widow of a hanged rebel.'

'You may be right,' she agreed. 'For the moment at least, I'll go along with you.'

He smiled, thinking he had won and they rode on in silence until a little later they reached the spot where the Redcoats waited in ambush. With an uplifted arm, the factor stopped her some distance away.

'Captain Brown—Captain Brown,' he shouted. 'Don't shoot—it's Campbell Frazer.'

Almost at once the officer stepped out of hiding and waited impassively on the road for them to join him. 'Well,' he asked, 'where's this rebel you promised us? I don't take kindly to being brought out on a wild goose chase Mr Frazer.'

'It's no wild goose chase as you put it. Haven't I captured the man himself already?'

The officer's eyes moved to Caro. 'Who's this?' he asked.

'Craigraven's wife,' the factor answered quickly before she could reply, moving between them. 'She's with us and party to this affair.'

Caroline flushed at the contempt in the Redcoat's eyes before he turned away to give orders to his men, who had come out of concealment. Campbell Frazer was careful to keep between her and the English officer and even if she had wanted, private speech with him would have been impossible.

The soldiers' horses were brought out of hiding and the men mounted quickly, eager to find the rebel and carry him back to Inverness as their prisoner. Caro rode with them, the factor by her side. As they drew near the place where Alan MacKenzie had been left, her heart began to leap and bound against her tight bodice and the cold perspiration of anticipation broke out on her skin.

Giving a wild Highland yell of triumph, Campbell Frazer charged forward, shaking the reins and kicking his pony in his eagerness. As he reached the spot where Craigraven had been Caro saw him stop in astonishment and spin the garron round in a tight circle as he stared wildly about him. Realising something was wrong the soldiers drew to a halt, looking round suspiciously, suspecting an ambush. The officer spurred his horse forward, snatching at the factor's bridle.

'Where's the man you promised?'

'He was here—we left him bound hand and foot. Didn't I make her tie him myself—' With the words suspicion dawned and his gaze flew to the watching English girl.

'Captain Brown—a word, if you please,' called Caro, seizing the opportunity.

Her cool English voice attracted the officer's attention and flinging his reins to a soldier, he dismounted, walking across to her, his heavy black riding boots flapping against his thighs.

'At your service, mistress,' he said with a slight bow.

'I am General Candover's niece,' Caro told him. Looking down she saw that he knew of her abduction and was waiting to hear more. Glancing significantly over his shoulder to where the bewildered factor was still searching for the missing Craigraven, she went on quietly. 'Let us go away a little— I have something to tell you.'

Allowing him to aid her to dismount, she accepted his arm as they left the group of interested soldiers. Not until they were out of earshot did she speak. 'The poor man is crazed, of course,' she said, seating herself.

A pair of shrewd eyes studied her. 'He called you Craigraven's wife,' he said, 'and yet the story is that you were taken against your will in mistake for the General's daughter.'

Caroline looked down and did her best to smile in a manner she had often seen Georgina use successfully. 'My uncle is a stern disciplinarian, Captain—I am not the first female who needed to use a little guile.'

'I—see.'

He looked unconvinced and she hurried on: 'I can assure you that I am very happily married, but this man who has contacted you, is somewhat . . . strange and has convinced himself that my husband is a Jacobite. I'm afraid that the factor has a grudge against him and it shows itself in this way. In reality we had ridden out with Craigraven's sister and Lieutenant James Preston, who is recovering from an accident.'

The soldier looked thoughtful. 'Jamie Preston has had leave of absence for some days, I know—also that his Commander was becoming worried that he had not returned.'

'We have been nursing him, until he was well enough to attempt the journey. He and Christian MacKenzie are a few miles back. I and the factor rode ahead, expecting to meet you. I had no idea that Campbell Frazer had told you such a strange tale.'

'The man must be half-witted! He wrote us that Craigraven had abducted you, in order to use you as a hostage for his brother's freedom.'

Caro shook her head sadly. 'His envy of my husband's inheritance and position has played upon his mind, I fear. His jealousy can be understood, but not his treachery.'

'So what do you want us to do? Take him back to Inverness with us?'

Caro shook her head. 'Now we understand his devious nature, he will be harmless, but if you could collect Jamie Preston and Christian I'd be grateful.'

'And you, mistress?'

She hesitated, before making up her mind. 'I will return to Craigraven Tower,' she said firmly. 'Pray explain all to my uncle and give my love to Georgina.'

Sensing that she had not told him the whole truth, the soldier searched her face. 'You are quite sure—shall I take you back to this tower of yours?'

She smiled gratefully, but shook her head. 'You are kind, but no—I'll not take longer of your time. Lieutenant Preston and Miss MacKenzie will be worried at being left alone so long. If I could leave them in your care, I will be more than grateful. They are only a short way behind and once you are on the main road, then it should not take you long to reach Inverness.'

'She's lying—can you no see that!' burst out the factor, facing them angrily, his hands clenched at his sides. 'Are you a fool man, to believe such nonsense. Craigraven's a traitor, I'm telling you—'

'Oh, Campbell, be quiet,' urged Caro in a weary voice. 'Can't you see that you're doing yourself no good?' She turned to the watching officer. 'Captain, *must* we listen to this farradale of a story?'

Campbell Frazer shook his head in frustration. 'She must have let him go,' he cried suddenly. 'I thought she was on my side, but really she must have tied the knots so loosely that he freed himself.'

Looking up at the English soldier Caro spread her arms wide. 'There *was* no one here,' she insisted. 'The poor man's deranged.

The factor ground his teeth audibly. 'He's somewhere around—look for him.'

'Campbell,' said the English girl in a commanding voice, 'you do yourself no good— carry on in this way and Captain Brown will have no choice but to carry *you* away.'

The officer had been watching her

thoughtfully. 'I have your word that Mr MacKenzie is no traitor?' he asked quietly.

'I assure you that he intends no harm to the throne or government—I truly believe that his sincere wish is to live as a Highland gentleman, caring for his family and estate with no thought for politics.'

The soldier nodded, satisfied. 'I shall convey your messages to your kinsfolk,' he told her gravely, saluting, before calling his men together, he gave the order to move off.

Once the sound of hoof-beats and jingling of accoutrements had died away the waiting silence made Caro's back prickle with unease.

'You'd have been wiser to send me with them,' the factor said softly behind her.

It took all her resolution to turn and face him. He was nearer than she had expected and she took an involuntary step away. Thinking she was showing fright, he smiled and reached out to take hold of her, his expression wolfish with triumph.

'Turn round, black cur, or is it only women you are capable of facing?' taunted a familiar figure and Craigraven leaped down from a boulder, his soft brogues scarcely stirring the dust as he landed.

Slipping at once into a wary fighting

stance, Caro saw that he already held his dirk in one hand, the other held away from his body to give balance.

With a strange cry, half rage, half despair, Campbell Frazer flung himself towards his adversary. The men crouched, circling, looking for an opening in the other's defence, before leaping together their raised arms locked as each strained to aim a mortal blow with the tiny black knives.

Flattening herself against the face of the towering rock, her arms spread wide, Caro watched as her husband and the factor fought. Teeth bared, their faces beaded with sweat, they struggled for supremacy, using strength and cunning as well as learned skills. Suddenly, Campbell Frazer tripped, falling heavily with Craigraven on top of him and a dreadful gurgling cry rent the mountain air.

For what seemed an age to the watching girl, they both lay still. A hand to her mouth Caro crept forward, her heart beating wildly with fear at what she might find.

'Alan—A-*Alan*?' she whispered through stiff lips.

As she tentatively approached one figure stirred and to her overwhelming relief Craigraven levered himself to a kneeling position. Head hanging he struggled for breath, his chest heaving as he stretched forward to turn over the limp body of the factor.

'Campbell!' he exclaimed, his eyes on the black knife handle sticking out of the man's chest, held there by the factor's own hand.

As they stared down in horror the hand fell away heavily to lie, fingers curling upward, in the dust. Reluctantly Caro's gaze travelled up as if impelled by some irresistible force and to her surprise she found the factor's eyes open and staring at her. Slowly they travelled to Craigraven and a gleam of malice flickered briefly in their fading depths.

'I—wish it had been you, Alan MacKenzie—' he said weakly, his voice a thin thread of sound. His chest heaved painfully, bloodied froth appeared at his mouth and with a long sigh his eyes closed wearily.

Craigraven was still, his head bowed, one hand touching the dead man's shoulder. 'Oh, Campbell man, where did we go wrong? When did we become enemies?' he asked bitterly.

'He was always your enemy,' Caro said quietly. 'He told me he hated you from the moment he and his mother came to the keep.'

Slowly Alan MacKenzie turned his fair

head until his gaze met hers, his brow furrowed.

'I had forgotten you, wife,' he said, in a tone that made the English girl draw back. 'You have much to answer for.'

As he rose to his feet and came towards her, she found herself backing away until brought up against the same rocky wall that had barred her way before.

'Wh-what happened to Rory?' she asked, hoping to divert him.

'He's safe away—we managed to snatch him from his guards as he was being taken to hear sentence. He's on the high seas to France now, with Johnnie to care for him.'

'I'm glad,' she said simply.

He eyed her quietly, still a few paces from her and then walked the last steps that separated them, placing his hands flat on the rock face either side of her shoulders. Not liking being his prisoner Caro moved uneasily, turning her head aside to avoid his grey eyes.

'So—you and Campbell planned together to betray me!'

The accusation stung her into anger and she looked up quickly. 'You know I did not,' she cried indignantly. 'Would you have escaped if I had tied your hands and feet properly? You've me to thank that the factor's tale was not believed.'

'I'll do my thanking when you've explained what you are doing here in the first
place, when I left you safe in the tower.'

Her powers of invention seemed to vanish
under the steady grey gaze. 'I—' she began
weakly, before subsiding into silence, her
mind completely blank.

'Must I remind you that we are alone—
that I can persuade you to answer my questions in any way I choose?'

His voice was soft in her ear, his breath
stirring her hair and she shivered with a
strange unfamiliar fear. Knowing that she
must make the attempt now or the moment
and her impetus would be lost for ever, she
pushed against Alan MacKenzie's chest with
both hands and all her strength. Taken by
surprise he stepped back to keep his balance
and seizing the opportunity Caro slipped
under his outstretched arm. Lifting her skirts
high, she fled to where she had left her pony
and scrambling on to his back, kicked him
into activity.

Behind her she heard a shout but,
crouching low, took no notice, instead con-
centrating on keeping her seat as the little
animal, galvanised into unexpected action
by her urgings, scurried and skipped along
the rough hillside. His short legs were unfamiliar with such speed and she knew that in

forcing him to the verge of his capabilities she was courting disaster. The end came suddenly, in his headlong flight the garron plunged faster and faster down the hill, until completely out of control, he lost his footing, throwing his rider over his shoulder before falling himself.

A shrill scream of equine fear echoed in Caro's head as she flew through the air, landing heavily she rolled over and over down the mountainside. Shutting her eyes against the sickening succession of half-glimpsed images and objects that formed in a wild kaleidoscope of colour she clutched at anything that presented itself in an effort to stay her fall. At last she was brought up short by a boulder, landing against it with a thud that drove the breath from her body.

Scrambling to her feet she staggered around in a daze, before a clatter of hoofs and the sound of her shouted name brought her to her senses. Her pony had regained his feet and was already some distance away, intent upon leaving his rider as far behind as possible. Still dizzy from her fall she was dimly aware of a rider flinging himself from his mount and running towards her. Before she could move, her shoulders were seized and she was shaken violently.

218 MASTER OF CRAIGRAVEN

'Caro—Caro! I thought you were dead, you daft wee woman.'

'Do that, Craigraven, and I think I will be,' she answered closing her eyes against the gyrating world. Her head drooped forward, hanging on her neck like a flower and she rested her forehead against the blue material of his jacket.

She felt him stiffen into stillness, the thud of his heart beating against her ear, then slowly his grip on her shoulders loosened, changed, and his arms crept round her in a gentle, firm embrace. The feel of his chin resting against her hair was at once familiar and welcome.

'Why must we always fight?' she wondered, her voice muffled.

'Because you are a wilful, scheming, disobedient, stubborn creature.'

His tone belied the words and she looked up, her gaze tentative and enquiring. With a groan, he gathered her closer, lifting her off her feet and burying his face in her hair.

'Oh, lassie, lassie, when I thought I'd lost you, the heart died in me. Didn't I wish it was me lying back there and not Campbell Frazer.'

Slowly her arms crept round his neck, her fingers entwining themselves in the fair curls that had escaped from the confining black ribbon.

'It seemed an age before you came, after I'd got rid of the Redcoat Captain,' she confided. 'I knew you were around, I'd banked on you wanting to deal with the factor but—'

'Losh, wifie—it wasna the factor I wanted to deal with. Didn't I want a word or two with you! After listening to that tale you spun yon poor wee mannie, I began to doubt my own senses.'

'It was all I could think of on the spur of the moment.'

'It didn't explain why you'd left the tower,' Craigraven said soberly, discarding the broad Scots accent.

Caro hid her face, 'Could—could I stay there after what had passed between us?' she asked in a whisper. 'We said such things—'

'We both own tempers, my lass—if I hurt you, then I'm sorry. Many's the time I nearly turned around on the road to Inverness. If it hadn't been for Rory and time running out, I'd have come back just to kiss away your tears.'

Caro raised her head and seeing the silver tracks glistening on her cheeks, Craigraven bent his own tall head to touch his lips to her face. Responding to the featherlight caress

Caro lifted her mouth to his and their kiss became an expression of love that lingered and clung and deepened.

'Oh, Alan MacKenzie, we've been such fools,' Caro exclaimed huskily, when at last their mouths parted.

'And will be again, I dare say,' he told her cheerfully, his eyes alight with an emotion that filled her with joy. With a gentle finger he touched her face, smoothing the fine arch of her brows, sliding down her nose and outlining the soft curves of her mouth. 'Light of my heart,' he said deeply, 'I love you.'

She caught his hand and rubbed her cheek against the hollowed palm. 'Take me home, dear husband,' she whispered.

A little later when the garrons had been caught and they were on their way to the tower, Alan MacKenzie turned to her.

'I had forgot,' he exclaimed, 'What's this about Christian and that Redcoat Lieutenant of yours?'

'He's not mine,' Caro returned demurely. 'He and your sister discovered a deep affection for each other while she nursed him. They were convinced that you would oppose the match and when I . . . decided that a loveless marriage was not for me, they thought it best to leave as well.' She looked at her companion anxiously. 'I do assure you that Jamie Preston is a man of honour. He will wed your sister at the first opportunity.'

Craigraven smiled. 'That I doubt not—and knowing my sister I am sure that she will persuade him to her convictions and make a good Jacobite out of him within a twelvemonth. It's well-known that women change their husbands.'

Caro looked at him, her eyes dancing. 'Is that so?' she teased.

Throwing back his head he laughed. 'I'm a changed man already—love can soothe a wild cat, so I've heard, *ghoal mo chridhe*.'

Her eyes widened. 'You said you'd call me that,' she breathed.

'Light of my life, dear white heart, I'll teach you the Gaelic and we'll spend the nights whispering love names to each other.'

'Alan MacKenzie, Master of Craigraven, I love you,' she breathed.

Brown fingers closed over the hand she held out and together they turned and rode on towards the waiting tower of Craigraven Keep.